LETHAL

USA TODAY BESTSELLING AUTHOR
TAYA RUNE

Cover Design: Sweet 15 Designs
For information contact :
purplerealmpublishing@gmail.com
ISBN: 978-1-922604-21-7 (ebook)
ISBN : 978-1-922604-22-4 (paperback)
ISBN : 978-1-922604-39-2 (audio)
First Edition: November 2022

Purple Realm Publishing

RIGHT TO RULE SERIES

USA TODAY BESTSELLING AUTHOR

TAYA RUNE

Purple Realm

PUBLISHING

Taya's Steamy Books

Steamy Contemporary

Champagne Resolutions

War of Hearts

Bewitching Twisted Fairytales

The Charming Thief

Fantasy Romance

The Right To Rule Series

Outcast

Lethal

Fatal

Betrayal

Denial
(Coming January 2024)

<u>Paranormal Mystery Romance</u>
Enchanted Underworld
Weapons of the Fae Queen Series

The Warlock's Lair

The Oracle's Court

The Nymph's Realm

The Dragon's Garden
(Coming 2nd November 2023)

Check out her website for all her current works.

tayarune.com

Newsletter

To receive up-to-date information, news and exclusive
offers online please sign up for the
Taya Rune newsletter.

https://www.tayarune.com/subscribe

Content Warning

If you are concerned about content, please check Taya's website for a list of warnings for all of her books.
It can be found under the 'Books' tab.

tayarune.com

For my mother
Thank you
Love you
Miss you

Prologue

Zussya

"Are you ready?" the heavy-set Brother of the Order of Seggar asked in his usual brisk fashion as he hurried toward the figure who knelt in contemplation at the altar of the old, almost-forgotten family chapel. The small house of worship had fallen into disuse as the palace grounds, as well as the royal family, had grown. Now it was an old relic that only a few visited.

"Yes," the hooded figure responded in a deep voice that almost rumbled like thunder. He stood slowly, but kept his head covered.

The Arch Deacon turned to the soldier standing at the chapel entrance. "Come along."

Both the soldier and the hooded figure followed the Brother out of a back door, and they hurried under the cover of the fading light to a side entrance that only the servants used. It would lead them through several food storage areas, and eventually to a large chamber filled with wheels of cheese that no one cared about—bar the palace cheese maker.

As they entered the cheese cellar, the Arch Deacon turned to the soldier. "Wait here," he ordered. "No one comes through. Yell if there is trouble." He handed him one of the two burning torches that he had collected as they entered the dimly lit section of the storage areas.

The soldier saluted, took up his position without comment while holding his flaming torch aloft, and left the other two to proceed further into the cheese chamber. The cheese cellar was larger than Arch Deacon Zussya remembered, and it took them a few minutes to get to the circular hidden room. He pushed open the ancient door and was surprised to see the huge round cauldrons lit. He paused in the doorway, blocking the entrance so the hooded figure couldn't enter, and peered into the secret room, suspicious. There were only three people who knew about this room and two of them lived on another world. Zussya looked to the far wall and to the stone arch that was typically filled with the brands of the Segar, only to find the brands had been activated and the usually plain stone wall shimmered softly, like sunlight bouncing off a still lake.

"Come in and close the door," a male voice with a slightly skewed accent spoke from the corner.

The Arch Deacon smiled; even though the accent was not quite the same, he would recognize the natural command in that voice anywhere. He stepped through the door and moved aside for the hooded man to follow. Quietly, he closed the door. "Did you bring that gorgeous wife of yours with you?"

There was a light chuckle. "Do you think me insane? I was never going to risk bringing her anywhere near the queens. She says we can trust the heir, but I will be my own judge of that."

The tall, silent man moved out from behind the Arch Deacon and pulled his hood down to reveal a strong face with a cleft chin and a high forehead. "You speak about my mother like that?"

"Yes, I do." The man in the corner stepped out of the light to reveal himself. "And I will continue to. I am unsure as to what you have been told, but there is one thing you need to understand before we proceed any further, my prince. I do not lie and I will not hold back to spare your feelings or because of your title."

Zussya laughed loudly and moved around the prince. "It is good to see you, my friend." The two men embraced and slapped each other on the back. "Plain speaking is exactly what the prince needs. I fear his mother has been filling his head with as many half-truths as Darria has with her offspring. I have done all that your wife has instructed over the years."

The young prince appeared to bristle at the conversation but remained silent.

"May I formally introduce you to the heir to the throne of Segarris, the first born son of King Tommofey, Prince Harlonngraith."

"It is an honor to meet you, Your Highness." The stranger bowed sincerely, all traces of harshness gone from his voice, and respect only remained. "I have waited for this moment a long time. I hope to serve you in the best way I know how and complete your training while you search for your Champion."

Prince Harlonngraith inclined his head as Arch Deacon continued the introductions. "This is the man your mother curses while secretly longing for him to return and help put everything right. She does not understand that he still works behind the scenes for her and the greater good."

The prince raised an eyebrow. "You are Captain Evannderth, also a Lord of the court? Bonded to the Seer of the Pomaikka?"

"Yes," Evannderth answered simply.

"You left my mother in great need. You were sworn to her service."

"There are things you and she do not understand, not even our mutual friend, the Arch Deacon, knows the full reasons we had to leave, but all will be revealed." Evan looked up at the prince. "You are going to need to make a choice right now. To face the challenge that has been issued and earn the right to rule you need to find your Champion, and I can tell you with utmost certainty that they do not live in this world, but in the world I live on. My wife, Kahlahnni, the fabled Seer, has lost much of her abilities but this she knows. You will need to trust me, if you come with me, and respect my conditions and choices."

Prince Harlonngraith looked to Arch Deacon Zussya, his face losing its bravado and showing the scared and confused young man underneath. He had the weight of a nation on his shoulders, and one wrong decision would cost him everything. Once a challenge was issued for the throne, the heir and the one who challenged the claim had half a year to find their fated Champion and arrive at the Arena at the dawning of the day to settle the issue. The Champions would fight to the death in single combat with minimal armour and the weapon of their choice. The winner then claimed the right to rule while the loser was executed immediately to join their Champion on the road to the afterlife.

"Your Highness, I can only tell you that I brought you here to meet Captain Evannderth, and that I trust him and the Seer more than any other person. I honestly believe they want the best for their nation of birth, even though they were driven from their home. I sent you to the Pomaikka on Kahlahnni's recommendation and that was a wise choice, just as your brother came to the church to be taught." Zussya halted his speech. "You are the prince and whatever you choose I will abide by and support you, but I urge you to follow your instincts and dismiss any negative words your mother has spoken about the captain and the seer."

The room stilled, but only for a moment.

Evannderth looked at something on his wrist, but he pulled his sleeve back down to cover it before Zussya could get a proper look. "There is no time to waste; the portal will only stay open for a few more minutes." The captain grasped Zussya's hand and looked him in the eye. "Be well, old friend. I have a feeling our paths will cross again." He let go and turned to Harlonngraith. "Choose."

"I will come with you to find my Champion. I wish to also learn more of what has been kept secret from me, and to meet the Gifted one."

"Good—" He paused. "There is one thing. We are going to have to do something about your name. I am simply Evan and Kahlahnni is known as Lahnni. How do you feel about the name Harley?"

"I don't like it, but I understand the need to not be known."

"Where we go there are no royal families with true power like you carry, and claiming to be royal will only cause headaches. I hope you have an open mind because it is about to be expanded quickly."

Evan moved toward the shimmering glow in the archway.

Zussya looked at the young man he had done everything in his power to keep alive and find ways to raise to be a good man in spite of his mother's demands and desire to have a son that allowed her to dominate him. He had tried to make sure the boy was well-rounded in his studies and had been exposed to many experiences, as well as trained in combat to protect himself. Now it was time to let Harlonngraith go and Zussya couldn't think of better people to hand over stewardship to than Evan and Lahnni. His final silent prayer as he bowed deeply to his prince was that the Champion Evan claimed lived through the portal was truly lethal enough to win. Surprisingly, Harlonngraith threw his proper training aside and leaned down to embrace the Arch Deacon. "Thank you for all you do for my family. You serve us well and

I am grateful for your prayers and guidance." With those parting words, the prince strode toward Evannderth; and without a backward glance, followed the captain through the shimmering wall.

Zussya stood there for several seconds and watched as the light changed and separated to become individual glowing brands that spun in a circle that's speed was slowly decreasing. The brands began to fade and settled into their permanent places on the wall. All eight brands were represented, which was always unusual. Typically, the Monarch and Gifted brands weren't displayed. The Monarch was only worn by one person at a time, and Lahnni was the only one to wear the Gifted brand in the last three generations. As the brands returned to normal, the fires in the huge cauldrons went out and the ancient, secret room was filled with shadows as the only light that remained was the flickering of the torch Zussya had carried in.

Quickly, he took up the torch, closed the door, and made his way back to the guard he had left at the entrance of the cheese cellar. "Put your hood up," he told the tall man. The soldier was six foot, six inches, and broad across the shoulders with light toned skin and lighter hair and eyes, much like the prince. "Walk with a little more swagger," Zussya explained.

"Swagger?" Your Excellency?" The man sounded surprised.

"Yes, swagger. The prince walks with a little more finesse."

"I'll do my best," he agreed but sounded doubtful.

"Keep your hood up unless you are in the prince's tent, and stay out of sight as much as possible. Ride in the middle of the troop. We need to keep this facade up as long as we can."

They hurried down the corridors, leaving the burning torch behind as they went back to the chapel and rushed through the building to come out the entrance to find the troop of palace guards milling about with their horses, still waiting on the prince to finish his prayers before heading out on his journey to find his Champion now that the Challenge had been issued. Arch Deacon made a show of bowing to the pretend prince as he mounted the grand stallion he always rode and headed out in the midst of his most loyal personal guards.

Zussya watched them ride out until the area was completely quiet. He took a deep breath and reached into the hidden pocket in his cassock and withdrew a letter he had been keeping for the past eighteen years. The Arch Deacon walked slowly now, taking his time as he peered into the surrounding darkness and made his way to the servants' entrance and out through the gate. There, just as he had hoped, was a man leaning against the wall resting his hand on an ornate walking cane, just out of reach of the light of the lamps that hung from the palace walls. It was now time to deliver the letter.

Chapter 1

Samarra

Mornings were usually the favorite time of Marra's day. The quiet moments before you started your never-ending to-do list. A chance to re-set your attitude and embrace a new start. But today felt different—heavy. She hadn't been sleeping well the last few weeks, and it was beginning to wear on her. Moving slowly through her morning exercises, her breath coming out as steam as she exhaled fully while completing her final kata, Marra tried to settle her errant thoughts. It was like the world had stopped and was holding its breath. It felt like she was waiting, but for what, Marra couldn't fathom.

Her life was full—complete. She lived with her parents on the outskirts of Melbourne, at the foot of a mountain range where they had carved their own piece of paradise after they had escaped their homeland. This was only months before Marra had been born, eighteen years ago. One of the first things her father had done was create a contemplation glade for him to spend time in, usually at sunrise, while her mother was often found sitting quietly by the small pond within the large private glade at sunset.

In many ways her parents were like the ying and yang symbol. Opposites that together made a perfect whole. Her father was tall, blonde, with eyes the color of the ocean—strangers often assumed him to be from some Nordic area in Europe. Marra's mother was darker in coloring; she had long, curly dark brown hair, rich chocolate brown eyes, and an olive skin tone, and was much shorter than her husband. People most often thought she came from Egypt or somewhere near there. Marra was a combination of both her parents: she was far taller than her mother, but still a hint shorter than her father. She had deep brown eyes but had much lighter hair coloring and her skin was fair in winter but tanned quickly in the harsh Australian summer.

The feeling of waiting weighed heavily on her as she brought her arms down to her sides and returned her feet to a relaxed position after finishing the last kata for the morning. She closed her eyes and took in one final deep breath, inhaling through her nose for three counts, holding it for two counts, and then exhaling with force for five counts. Usually this would be enough to clear her restless thoughts, but it seemed that today they had a tighter grip. Perhaps fifteen minutes of free writing would help.

Marra slipped her puffer jacket on over her sweats and grabbed her bottle of water before picking up her small tote bag that held her notepad and pen as well as a breakfast bar—for just these moments. She left the small patch of perfectly manicured lawn and walked slowly along the cobbled path, in between small shrubs and solar garden lights to the pond that brought her mother peace. The pond was completely man-made and was fed by a small solar powered fountain. Next to the pond was a carved stone bench seat, surrounded with flowering plants of white. On the opposite side of the pond stood a beautiful sculpture of a woman carved from the blackest stone. She was covered in a hooded cloak that looked to be made of feathers, and she carried a newborn in her arms protectively. The hood covered her face, so you could only ever see shadows, but when Marra was younger she had often dreamed of the statue coming to life and revealing the woman as her mother. It was a silly dream, and she wondered at times what it represented.

After taking a long drink from her water bottle, Marra pulled the notepad and pen out of her bag, smiled fondly at the statue, and sat on the bench. She let her mind wander and her thoughts flow onto the page. As a writer, sometimes this was a perfect way to be rid of stray ideas before you turned your full focus onto your current man-uscript—Marra had always found it particularly helpful when she was stuck on a scene. Disjointed words filled her mind, and she wrote them down, not truly taking any notice of where it was leading her.

Marra heard the footsteps approach much earlier than when he made his presence known. She didn't startle at all when he coughed to announce his arrival. "Hi, Dad." She looked up from her writing.

"Good morning, Faffia. Am I interrupting you?"

"Never."

"Did you sleep well?" he asked. He always asked that question.

Marra shrugged, as she did most mornings. Her sleep was rarely restful, but she barely remembered her dreams. The only times she slept fully was when her mother sang her to sleep. Her mother claimed it was an ancient lullaby but did not know where it came from. At eighteen, Marra felt it silly to ask her mother to sing her to sleep, so instead struggled with her nocturnal issues without complaint.

Her father reached out his hand and rested it gently on her head for a moment. "You look tired."

Marra frowned; no woman ever appreciated being told she looked tired.

"Your mother and I have been talking and we are concerned that you are doing too much. You work hard at the dojo almost daily, while also helping with all the chores around here, and you stay up late to write your novel. You seem to have no time for fun."

"I love working at the dojo, and you know I want to be a writer... That is my fun—" she said, but he interrupted.

"We know, which is why we think you should take a break from teaching and focus on your writing. We still expect you to do your chores, but we want you to go out and have fun with your friends, live your life, and focus on the things you love."

Marra frowned as she processed his words. "But that leaves you to take care of everything at the dojo and we are too big for you to do that. I knew what I was agreeing to when we took on the extra students and opened up to day classes for self-defense."

"I have someone coming into teach for a month. He needs the added training from me but is fully capable of taking care of the kids and the self-defense classes. I will take on all the advanced adult classes but have a feeling he will be up for that challenge too in a few weeks. He has been trained by the best, as far as I understand."

"Why didn't you tell me before now?"

"I didn't know he was coming until a few days ago. It has been something that might happen, but we weren't sure it was required until recently."

"Okay," Marra said hesitantly. "If you are sure he is up for the task."

"Yes, he received his training from the same people I did, though I have a feeling they may have gone a little easier on him than me."

She cocked her head to the side, a habit she had picked up years prior when she was thinking. "Why is that?"

"I'll explain it all, but not today." He reached out and again caressed her head. "Your mother has breakfast ready. I am going into the dojo early to run him through a few things, but as of today, you are free to do what you wish for four weeks. Write, read, party with your friends. I want to see some serious progress on that manuscript the next time I ask."

Marra stood, letting her notepad and pen fall to the ground. She embraced her father and kissed his cheek. "Thank you, Dad."

"You are welcome, Faffia."

She smiled and stepped back, her face showing nothing but gratitude while her mind tried to process why the sudden about face on her responsibilities? Marra had always been raised to understand responsibilities were something you never became slack about. Was something wrong and they didn't want to tell her? That feeling of heaviness was back.

"Don't be too much longer out here. Your mother has left for work, and your breakfast will get cold."

"Mum left already? Today is full of surprises."

Her father laughed. "I guess it is. Mum had a feeling she would need to be at the shop early. You know how she gets with her feelings... No one stands in her way."

Marra laughed too, some of her tension easing. Her mother had always been known for her instincts—it's how she had come to own a small shop in a set of strip shops that specialized in healing crystals and tarot card readings. When she had a "feeling" and voiced it, Marra had come to understand that she should never ignore it. "I'll be there in a minute. Thank you for giving me this time to write. I promise I won't let my training stop."

"Never expected you to. After all, you are my daughter." And with those words he walked away from her.

She plonked down on the bench and absently picked up her notepad and pen, pondering what she would do first with all this free time she had just been given. Oh, *stop pretending,* she told herself. *You know exactly what you are going to do. You are going to go inside and eat your breakfast and take a long shower before you spend the whole day in your favorite pair of pj's and finish the outline of your novel that you have been hoping for weeks to find time for. And you are going to text a few of your friends and see who can do breakfast on Saturday because for the first time in forever you have the morning off.*

Marra pushed the idea that something wasn't quite right further away and ignored her earlier feelings of waiting and gathered up her things. As she folded the cover of her notepad over, a word that she had written from her free writing session earlier that morning jumped out at her as it was repeated many times on the single page. Moehanne. Marra studied it for a moment and tried to understand what it meant. She had been taught her mother's people's language and it was the language they used as they sat around the dinner table at night—her parents insisted they keep in practice though she had never meet anyone else who spoke it. Yet this word was one she had never learned, but it resonated with her in a way no other word did

"Moehanne." She said the word aloud as she headed to the entrance, and if she believed in omens she would have been spooked as a gust of wind swept the protected contemplation glade and rustled the leaves in the large tree that hung over the statue of the feather-cloaked woman and child.

Chapter 2

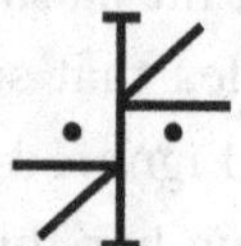

Harlonngraith

Prince Harlonngraith had never felt so alone, and he was surprised to find he enjoyed it. No one bothered him, no one knew him, he was just another foreigner in this strange city. There was so much to see and understand that his mind had quickly decided that in order for him not to go crazy he would just have to accept many things without understanding the why of it. It was not in his nature, nor what he was brought up to do as a leader, but it was something he was adjusting to. He had to put his complete faith in a stranger and hope that the choices he made were the right ones or Harlonngraith's life would end as would all his hopes and dreams for his country. He had risked everything to follow the Captain into the portal, and prayed every night that it had been the right decision. So far he had not been introduced to his Champion and it weighed heavily on him.

There was a polite knock on the door, and he stopped himself from responding with a command to enter and instead stood and made his way to the door and opened it. Captain Evannderth stood there, holding several large bags. "Here." He shoved the bags in the prince's direction. "I guessed the sizes as best I could. Go and change, and also try on the ghi. We have your first class in an hour."

Harlonngraith blinked at him. What was he talking about? "Class?" he asked.

"Yes, class. We are down an instructor for a month and I want to see what you know."

Harlonngraith bristled. He had been taught by the best instructors at both the palace and within the Pomaikka. "I am considered to be one of the best."

Evan looked at him sternly. "Can we step out of the hallway, please?"

Harlonngraith moved back into the small apartment Evannderth had set up for him prior to his arrival. He dumped the three large bags of clothes on the small kitchen benchtop. "I am here to find my Champion, not to take classes. I need to find out if he is ready for what is to come. This is not about me."

"Ah, and that is where you are wrong, Your Highness. It is all about you. You are here to find that one person who is fated to fight to the death for you. Are you worth that sacrifice?" Evan's piercing blue eyes were commanding.

Harlonngraith met the gaze from his superior height, but the captain was unfazed, which Harlonngraith should have expected. "I think I will make a good king. Segarris needs a strong king who will lead them to peace. I am versed in all I need to be. And I can take care of myself on a battlefield if it comes to war."

"That remains to be seen. You will meet your Champion when I deem you ready and worthy. At the moment, all I see is a young man who is far too impressed with telling me rather than showing me who he is."

"I speak the truth." Harlonngraith was not used to having his word questioned, and he was not enjoying the experience.

"You speak the truth as far as you know it, lad. You have been trained by men I trained. I have no doubt you are good, but were they ever easy on you because of your station or on your mother's orders?"

That gave Harlonngraith pause. That had never, not once, crossed his mind. What would happen if it were true? "I also studied with the Pomaikka." He said the words proudly. "I was considered accomplished amongst them."

"Again, I would question who trained you within their ranks."

It suddenly dawned on Harlonngraith what Evannderth was really implying. Had he been trained by the best and could he compete with the best? Or was he only ever given opponents he could beat or would challenge him just enough? He didn't like the idea, but he could not deny it. "I will try on the clothes," he said, rather than argue any further. He thought he saw a moment of respect cross the handsome older man's face. Harlonngraith had clearly passed a test of some kind.

He picked up the bags and went to his bedroom. It was sparsely furnished with a large bed and twin bedside tables. He tossed the bags on the bed and dug through them to find clothing that were similar to Evannderth's. "The small, stretchy cloth pants with short legs are called briefs, and they go on first," Evannderth called from the other side of the door.

Harlonngraith scowled and opened the last bag to find what the captain was referring to as well the ghi. "If you put on the ghi first and then open the door, I can quickly give you a rundown on what the other items of clothing are called. It only occurred to me now that you would be as hopeless as I was when it comes to clothing."

"I think I can manage," Harlonngraith answered.

"Really? Great, then get dressed in briefs, jeans, socks, a t-shirt, and then sweater, and sneakers."

Harlonngraith's eyes narrowed at all the clothing, completely lost with all the names Evannderth had just spoken. He finished undressing and pulled on what he assumed were the briefs and then pulled on the only thing he knew was close enough to the ghi that he would typically train in and tied it up just as he would with the Pomaiika. He wrenched open the door. "You are testing me," he spoke plainly.

"Yes," admitted Evannderth.

"Why?"

"Because it is needed." Harlonngraith glared at him, which would have sent any of his subjects into an immediately submissive stance, but Evannderth just laughed. "It needs work. Raise your head a little and clench your jaw, so it looks like you are refraining from sending someone to their death."

He couldn't help it. Harlonngraith laughed. He stepped aside and allowed the older man into his room to explain all the different items of clothing on the bed. It didn't take long. Evannderth also took a few moments to explain what was acceptable to wear in public and what was worn within your own home. "I've left something in the car. Get changed and bring out your ghi." He looked at the thing on his wrist like he had in the secret room only two days ago. "Get a move on. We have to get to class, remember."

Harlonngraith waited for Evannderth to leave and then quickly took off the ghi and folded it respectfully. Even though he rarely folded his clothes, he knew to take care of this possession. After studying the array of clothes for a few moments longer, he chose what Evannderth had suggested: jeans, t-shirt, and the sweater. They felt odd, but comfortable, though he did have a moment of frustration when he couldn't figure out how to do up the jeans' closing area. What he was shocked with was how remarkably comfortable the things called sneakers were. He felt like his feet were walking on clouds.

Carrying his ghi out into the main room of his apartment, Harlonngraith found Evannderth holding a bag and a dark cloak over his arm. "This is a backpack. It has more pockets than the ones back home, and this is like a cross between a jacket and a cloak. It is called a trench coat and my wife assures me that with your height and build you will look almost kingly in it." Before Harlonngraith could say anything, Evannderth went on. "Put your ghi in your backpack and get your key that I gave you the other day. We will walk to the dojo so you can learn the way when it comes time to do it on your own."

"On my own?"

"Yes, you will run several classes a week and train with the adults twice a week and me personally once a week. Our normal instructor is off for a month on personal leave. You and I will pick up all the classes they taught. This way you earn your keep while you are here, and I get to see if you are as good as you claim."

Harlonngraith wanted to ask how he was supposed to find his Champion if all he was doing was teaching classes, but something stopped him. He now needed to know, just for his ego, and he hated to admit it, but had his instructors been going easy on him all this time?

"Now, don't forget you must simply call me Evan."

"Yes, and I am to be known as Harley."

Chapter 3

Samarra

The fifteen boys and girls ranging from ages eight to twelve giggled and waved as she opened the door and entered the dojo. Marra held her finger up to her lip to tell them to be quiet and then indicated they needed to turn around and watch their teacher. She hurried over to the small group of parents that watched and chatted in a group in the corner of the room. "Hi," she spoke quietly to two of the mums.

They returned the greeting with friendly smiles.

Marra turned and watched the new instructor adjust the small foot of one of the children as they practiced their blocking moves. He straightened and Marra's eyes widened at the tall, broad man that flicked his eyes in her direction before he was drawn back to one of the children who was spinning in place rather than following what the others were doing. Marra smiled to herself; she loved Elijah's carefree attitude, but it had taken her months to figure out ways to keep him focused in class.

"What are you doing?" the replacement instructor asked in a voice that rumbled like thunder and for some reason made Marra's insides melt at the thought of him whispering to her with that voice. She had been clearly reading too many romance novels for that to be the first thing she thought of.

She watched Elijah stop and gulp as he looked up, craning his neck to meet the instructor's gaze. "I'm twirling," he said, as if it should be obvious what he was doing.

"Could you please stop and return to the assigned exercises?" the man rumbled at him.

"It's boring. I wanna twirl," Elijah said stubbornly.

The man crossed his arms over his impressive chest and Marra waited. He was stiff and formal, and this would not put the children at ease. "I understand that spinning is fun, but it will not help you learn to block."

Marra watched as the children, one by one, stopped what they were doing and started to muck around, each distracting the next one. The unruly children grew louder, but the instructor seemed not to notice.

"Is your parent here?" he asked the small boy.

Elijah shook his head. Marra wanted to explain but she hesitated, and another parent spoke before she could. "Elijah lives with his grandmother, who drops him off here each Saturday while she does her grocery shopping."

"I see," he rumbled, and Marra's heart fluttered like some silly virgin. "Will she come in to collect him?"

"No, she waits in the car."

"Very well." He looked down at the boy who had now stopped spinning and was staring up at him with sad eyes. The man reached out and patted him awkwardly on the head. It was only then did he notice the mob of children carrying on behind him. "Be quiet and still," he spoke loudly and firmly, but only about half the children responded.

Marra bit her lip. She wanted to help, but she was only here to observe. She had no intention of interfering or revealing who she was. Truly she had only come because her two best friends at breakfast that morning had badgered her about who it was that had replaced her, and wasn't she the least bit curious? They had finished their breakfast, and on the way home, Marra had found herself driving to the dojo as if on autopilot. After a brief moment of feeling guilty, she decided to follow through with her friends' suggestion and check out the instructor who had appeared from nowhere.

She watched him glance up at the large analogue clock on the wall and frown, then his expression cleared on his handsome face. "We will do ten punches with each hand, then ten side-kicks with each foot, and that should end the lesson. I want the punches and kicks to be precise and powerful, and for you to count out each one. Start with your right hand," he spoke loudly and Marra melted a little more with the combination of his strong accent and deep voice. "And one," he started, not checking to see if the children were ready. Some began while others looked around, as if only now realizing what was happening. By the fourth count they had all fallen into line and were all punching the air enthusiastically.

The mother beside Marra sighed quietly but dramatically. "You are better with the children, but he is definitely something to appreciate," she murmured quietly.

Marra chuckled softly but didn't reply. She wasn't quite sure what she wanted to say anyway. He looked over to her again as he instructed the children to start kicking with their right foot and they all began to count loudly. It was a good technique she had not tried before. This kept them engaged in a different way. She would have to try it when she returned to the dojo.

He dismissed the class and moved to the back of the room, away from the parents, as if he didn't want to talk to anyone, and stood there sipping from his water bottle. This was Marra's moment to leave. She greeted several children who said hello to her and then Marra walked out with a group of parents. Hopefully he would assume she was another parent and have no need to tell her father that someone had turned up to just watch him.

Story ideas began to form in her head as she hurried back to her car, and Marra picked up her phone and opened the app she used to dictate while she drove to and from the dojo when inspiration struck. In the privacy of her own car and her own thoughts, she turned the car on and the radio down, and began to describe the man she had just drooled over. He was approximately six foot, seven inches tall, and broad of shoulder and chest, but not barrel chested. She took a moment to stop and wonder what he would be like naked, but that was not relevant to her story. After all, she wrote epic fantasy, not fantasy romance, so him with his shirt off was not something she needed to think about, but her mind and groin told her different. Marra described his heavy accent and almost guttural voice, as well as his somewhat stern demeanor, and the way he spoke to the children was almost like a commander rather than a teacher. Again, her mind wandered to him giving her orders in the bedroom and this time it made her flush. It had been clearly too long since her and her boyfriend had split up, and she was taking this fantasizing a little too far, but it wasn't hurting anyone and no one would know.

He would make a dashing knight in shining armor come to rescue a village from a marauding horde of goblins in one of her books. Or he could be someone running from his fate, hiding in the same village, and warring with himself whether to show his magical abilities to save the day or allow them all to die to keep his secret. The possibilities were endless, and she spent the rest of the trip home dictating all the different ideas that popped into her head.

By the time she got home, a proper idea had begun to form and she was excited to get into her room and start making a basic outline and create a character profile for her flawed hero.

Chapter 4

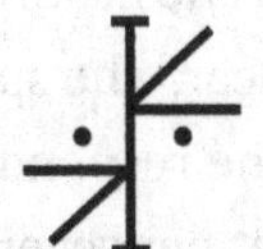

Harlonngraith

It was his second week teaching in this strange land and things had not improved greatly; Harlonngraith still struggled to get the children to listen. It didn't help that the woman who had been at the Saturday morning class was here again at the mid-week class, sitting in the corner, occasionally looking up at him. He found her very distracting. It was as if something about her called to him. If he wasn't so focused on not yelling at these children to behave, his body might betray him and show the world what the woman was doing to him.

It was about halfway through the forty-five-minute class, and he was exhausted already. Trying to keep the frustration from his voice, he called a drink break, and the children scattered to their parents or their bags to get their bottles. He watched surreptitiously and was surprised when no children went to the beautiful woman in the corner to get a drink. It was only after they had got their drinks that many of the children went to sit with her. She greeted them all by name and asked how their week had been. This made Harlonngraith frown for a moment before it all fell into place. This was the instructor he was replacing. Had she come to spy on him?

Before he could stop himself, he stalked toward her, the children scattered, and she hastily stood. "Hello," he said.

"May your path be clear," she spoke softly in greeting.

"And your life long," he responded out of habit, before stopping and blinking at her several times like one of the night birds.

"I am Harl—" He stopped himself from saying his full name. "I am Harley."

"I am Marra."

"She's our teacher," a child piped up.

"Why aren't you teaching, Marra?" another asked.

"Are you sick?" asked a little girl, her voice full of what he guessed was fear.

"No, no. I am just having a little holiday, but I missed you all and had to do paperwork for the place, so came to say hello." She smiled warmly at all the children, and they grinned back, Harlonngraith found himself smiling, too.

"Well, if you are not sick, perhaps you could join me in teaching this class?" he found himself asking.

"Oh no, I have no wish to intrude," she replied hastily, her eyes fluttered up to his face and then down to her feet.

His heart thudded in his chest at her soft voice. "You are not intruding. I think you would have noticed by now that I need some help. It is becoming clear to me that I have no idea how to control children."

The laugh that tumbled freely from her mouth was mesmerizing. No one laughed like that at him. His thoughts were quick to point out that it was perhaps that he never jested and made fun of himself like this. He was somewhat of a serious person—he had had to be. All the responsibility of being the heir to a large country with three provinces that could splinter apart at any time, and a war that broke out every decade or so on the Islands of Lebbograth, where his father had died, made one a little sour.

"Very well," she said. "I am happy to help."

"Great." Harlonngraith couldn't believe how much lighter he felt at her saying yes. He turned and gave the children his first genuine smile all class. "Marra will be joining us for the rest of the class."

There were a few children who whooped loudly, while others just smiled happily.

Without warning, Marra clapped in a sequence and the children immediately stopped their chattering and cheering and clapped in the same sequence in response. "How did you do that?" he asked, astounded.

"It's a trick. Most children are taught this when they first begin school. It is a way for the teachers to gain the attention of the class quickly."

"Clever," he commented.

"Okay, everyone in their assigned spots." She spoke in a clear tone, with a combination of command and cheerfulness.

Harlonngraith was sure he would never be able to master that combination. He watched with growing awe as she went on.

"You have all been very cheeky, but now it's time to show Harley how well-behaved and clever you are." Marra and Harley walked to the front of the large square mat where they did all their classes while the children lined up in their assigned spots. "This keeps the chatty ones separated, and the siblings who fight out of each other's way," she explained quietly to him.

He nodded, but said nothing. He watched her tie her hair up in a messy knot on top of her head in silence—even that simple gesture was breathtaking. Harlonngraith didn't get a chance to ogle further as Marra quickly took control and got them all to run around the edge of the mat, and then return to their spot and spin, just like Elijah had done in his first class. And then another sprint around the mat, and then more twirling, where this time he was expected to participate before she got them all to shake their legs and arms before settling into a relaxed position to receive their next instructions.

The rest of the class went quickly, and Harley began to enjoy himself. He was able to correct the children without losing control of the class, and even began giving a few words of encouragement to several of them. He was rewarded with wide smiles and a thumbs up from one of the dads who was watching the class.

Harlonngraith relaxed even further and was elated beyond proportion when a little girl wrapped her arms around his thigh at the end of the class and looked up at him and said thank you. He disengaged her small hands, bent down to her level, and smiled happily at her. "Thank you for working so hard. I will see you next week."

Several other children said goodbye, though there was no more hugging, and Harlonngraith felt for the first time since coming through the portal that he had achieved something. It had been a humbling week. First the disastrous classes with the children, then the self-defence class he had taught yesterday where the majority of women giggled and chatted almost as much as the children had. Then to complete the self-deflating week, Evannderth had given Harlonngraith his first private class and had put him through his paces. The prince had felt that he had performed well, but all he had got from the captain at the end of the gruelling session was a half nod and a muttered, "It's a start."

The dojo emptied out, and he watched Marra walk over to where she had been sitting in the corner earlier in the night to gather her things. He went to the front of the room and did the same. "I am happy to lock up," she said from her corner of the room.

"Thank you, but no. Evan has given me that responsibility."

He turned to find her slipping off her sneakers. He frowned. "What are you doing?"

"Challenging you." Her voice was soft.

"I'm sorry?" He was certain she had just said she was challenging him, but there was no way this woman, though tall at what he guessed was six foot, and clearly able to teach children the basics of their fighting techniques, really believed she would be able to best him. He didn't think Evannderth would be happy if he accidentally hurt his instructor.

She took off her thick sweater to reveal a tight black t-shirt underneath. He told himself it was rude to stare, but her curves were perfect. She wore some form of pants that were almost like a second skin. He had noticed that no men wore them and only some women. "I said I am challenging you." Her voice was firmer.

"I don't know if that is a good idea." He kept his eyes on her face. "I don't want to hurt you."

She laughed in an almost insulting way. "Let's use staffs. First to score three touches wins. What do you say?"

Harlonngraith slipped his shoes back off. "I think it is a bad idea, but I have been brought up to never back down from a warrior's challenge, so I say yes." He had decided that he would teach her a lesson and show her not to be silly by challenging men far more capable than her.

Marra smirked at him, and it took all his concentration not to move across the room and crush her body to his. She walked over to the wall that had a rack of varying lengths of staffs and chose one. Slowly, she returned to the center of the sparring floor and waited for him.

Samarra

A thrill ran through Marra as she waited for Harley to choose his staff or back down from the challenge. She hoped he didn't back down as she hadn't sparred in several weeks and she had never had the chance to fight someone as large as him. She couldn't quite believe how sassy and forward she had been. It was so unlike her. Maybe it was the familiar surroundings that had put her at ease enough to reveal the part of her she kept hidden.

She stood relaxed, conserving energy and staying focused on her opponent. After another few seconds of hesitation, Harley visibly shrugged and walked to the rack to choose his weapon. She had to admit she enjoyed watching him walk; there was something imposing about him. He carried himself in a way most men would find arrogant but she found appealing. To her it was a confidence in who he was, and she only wished one day to emulate that.

"You certain you want to do this?" he rumbled at her as he joined her on the mat.

"Having second thoughts?" she taunted. She couldn't help herself. There was something about him that brought out her flirtatious side. Maybe it's the fact they were in her domain for once and here was a man clearly stronger and taller than her. Most men she met were put off by both her strength and height.

"I don't want to hurt you."

"Aren't you afraid that I might hurt you?" she teased.

"No," he said the word bluntly.

It should have enraged her, but instead, she laughed. He had such an odd effect on her. Marra took a step back and moved into a crouching position. He joined her and mirrored her stance perfectly. A strange sensation ran through her body, and she moved to stand normally.

"What is wrong? Do you wish to not do this now?" He sounded confused and concerned.

Marra shook her head. "No, sorry, just a moment of déjà vu. I seem to be getting them more often than normal. It freaks me out sometimes." It took her by surprise that she was willing to admit that to him.

He stood upright now. "What is déjà vu?" he mispronounced the word badly, but she didn't correct him.

"It's a feeling a person gets like they have lived the moment before."

"And this happens often to you?"

"More than most people, I think. Or maybe they do not talk about it." She cocked her head to one side. "Does it ever happen to you?"

His brow furrowed, and she thought it made him look cute. "I don't think so."

Marra shrugged. The feeling had passed. "Oh well, it doesn't matter. Shall we?" She returned to her crouching position.

"If you are sure?" Harley moved to mirror her again.

"Let's do this." And with those words spoken, they began to circle each other.

Marra's heart pumped faster as adrenaline coursed through her. She feinted to strike twice to gage his reaction time; it was good, but not as good as hers. She studied the way he placed his feet and soon understood he truly had had very similar training to herself. This was going to be interesting, but she had every confidence that she could win.

The staffs rang out as they connected for the first time in a flurry of strikes and counter strikes. Marra ducked as the staff soared over her head, he had a much greater reach, but he had over-extended himself, she brought her own staff up and tapped him smartly on his outer ribs. He let out a satisfying oof.

"One," she said quietly, almost to herself.

They returned to circling each other, occasionally striking their staffs. Marra saw immediately that while his height gave him greater reach, it also gave him the disadvantage of having longer legs, and when he crossed his feet over to continue to circle an opponent, it would be an opportune moment to strike.

A small change in the position of his feet was the only warning Marra got as Harley launched a blitz attack, his staff whirling from hand to hand as he charged at her. She let him push her back for several steps before engaging. With practiced efficiency, Marra brought her staff up with perfect timing and halted his fancy twirling. He grunted with the unexpected impact but recovered quicker than she thought he would.

For some reason, it was important for Harley to like her and not see her as a show off, so Marra deliberately gave him an opportunity to score, and he did by tapping her upper arm with the staff. "One," he echoed her word from before, but he did it with a satisfied smirk.

Her arm stung a little, but he had most assuredly pulled his hit as to not hurt her. Marra didn't reply, instead, she decided to catch him off balance and keep the smirking to a minimum by feinting a hit to his side but switching the direction and grip on the staff and coming down on his foot that he had over extended and couldn't move in time. She returned his smirk with one of her own. "Two."

He grunted in response as they both moved apart and returned to their original crouching stances. "You want to keep going?" she teased.

"Fight," he demanded, and her insides heated.

"Very well," Marra said before launching an attack at his head. He counter-attacked and they spent several minutes trading blows with their staffs, and again, with reasons she didn't quite understand, she allowed Harley to hit her rather than easily block the sweeping movement.

"Two."

"Next hit wins."

For a further ten minutes, the two of them circled each other, the staffs clashing continually as one tried to get the upper hand and win the bet. With a resounding echo, their staffs connected, but neither retracted their weapon; instead, they held the staffs against each other. Marra knew he was stronger and would overpower her quickly, so stepped in closer to add all the strength she could, he mirrored the move, and they ended up facing each other, both panting heavily. She looked up at him, and lost focus of what they were doing for a split second as she discovered he had gorgeous gray eyes, like nothing she had seen before. Bringing herself back to the moment, Marra chose to wait and see what he would do.

She could easily win by tipping her staff a few inches, as without looking she knew her staff was bare centimeters from his shin; instead, she stilled and allowed him to do one of three things. He could call a truce, he could step back and continue to fight, or he could tip his own staff and touch her neck, which was the closest point on contact for him to hit. Whatever he chose would reveal much, and Marra was willing to lose this match to learn more about Harley as a person.

He held her gaze a moment longer before he tipped the tip of his staff forward a fraction and she felt it gently touch her neck. "Three," the word was barely a whisper. No gloating followed, just an inclination of his head before he stepped back and broke the moment.

"Congratulations," Marra said as she held out her hand to take the staff from him. "I'll just put these away and grab my stuff, and then you can lock up as promised."

"You fight very well," Harley complimented.

Marra waited a moment, expecting the typical "for a girl" back-handed ending, but it never came. "Thank you. So did you," she responded as she walked toward the rack.

"I will make a new deal with you." Harley moved to where his backpack leaned against the wall.

"Okay, let's hear it." Marra was curious.

"I will allow you to lock up if you come back and spar with me again. Deal?"

Marra's flirty ways abandoned her and suddenly she was the shy and awkward girl that she usually showed the world. She wanted to say something funny, or sexy, but instead, her voice went too high-pitched and she answered with a, "Yeah, sounds great." And even to her it sounded like she wasn't that enthused about it. Marra lowered her head to hide her flushed cheeks as she walked back across the mat to get her laptop and bag.

"After the little ones' class on Saturday afternoon?" he asked, his voice softer, but there was still that delicious rumble to it.

"Yes, that sounds good." Marra still wouldn't look up, instead choosing to focus on shoving the computer into its case.

There was silence for a few moments, and Marra wished she could be like her friends, who always had something witty to say. She thought of clever lines in her head, and could come up with them while writing, but saying them out loud was a step too far usually.

"Thank you again for the help earlier. I will see you soon." Harley finally filled the awkward silence before he walked out of the dojo.

"Bye," Marra said under her breath as the door swung shut. She looked up to see him watching from the window. She raised a hand to wave goodbye, which he returned with a nod of his head before he strode off.

Chapter 5

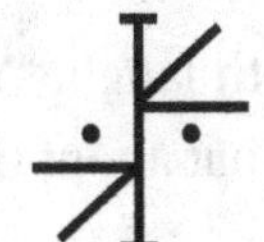

Harlonngraith

It was Friday night and Captain Evannderth had stopped by with something called pizza to talk about the week and check-in, as he put it. Harley had opened the door to find the older man standing there with a flat, square box in his hand. Whatever it was smelled good.

"I like pizza," Harley announced as he took another slice of the pepperoni pizza with all its golden cheese. It was his fifth slice.

Evan laughed. "I forget sometimes that you are not from here. You have adapted very well. It took me years to stop being surprised by everything."

"I have you to guide me. That has helped immensely."

Evannderth had done so much for him. Not only had he provided shelter and clothing, he had also brought food already prepared every three days to put in the thing called a fridge and had shown him how to heat it in the microwave. He had given him a small, thin card made from a strange substance and told him it was a credit card and had then taken him to a shop to show him how to use it if he needed to buy something. There were few gold coins here, most people used these card things. "I also like the thing called showers, and all the hot water that doesn't run out. A garderobe that doesn't smell, and the clothing you gave me."

This made Evannderth laugh. "Yes, they are all things that make life better. What about the stranger things, like cars, phones and tv's?"

"I decided that I would not be here long enough to learn all I need if I were to live here forever, so I will not worry about things I do not understand..." Harlonngraith paused. He wasn't sure how much further to push the conversation. He wanted to broach the subject of his Champion but felt that it was still off limits. He also want-ed to question him thoroughly on Marra, but for some reason, kept their meeting and subsequent sparring to himself. He wasn't sure how he felt about the beautiful woman. She had made an impact, but he was confused with her behavior. All he knew for certain was that any time his mind was idle, it returned to her soft smile, sparkling brown eyes, and strong, yet feminine body. It was a body he longed to touch, to hold. He could take her to bed and not worry about hurting her. The thought made him shift uncomfortably in his chair to hide his sudden erection.

"How do you feel about your half-brother challenging you to the throne?" Evannderth changed the topic.

This gave Harlonngraith pause. He was not used to people asking him such direct personal questions. As heir, he was treated like his word was already law. He was only ever asked questions regarding things to do with ruling the nation of Segarris. "I have not taken the time to give it much thought. I still hope that when we reach the Arena, I will find he has chosen to not follow through with the challenge, and instead, we may be able to find a way to co-exist."

"Do you think that's likely?"

"No," Harlonngraith admitted. "To be honest, I find the entire situation frustrating. I should have been on the throne for the past three years, making plans, improving the army, making certain our people were cared for. Instead, the country has languished as the council debates every decision and my vote is just one of many. Though my opinions hold sway, it is still just one voice at the moment. All because Darria"—he almost spat out his Aunt's name—"wanted to retake what she had lost, and didn't care who she hurt to do it."

Evannderth nodded but didn't interrupt.

"I am led to believe that she was one of the main reasons you left Segarris. Arch Deacon Zussya says Darria would have caged the Seer for her abilities and never given her her freedom."

"She did do that," admitted Evannderth, his voice quiet, regretful. Harlonngraith wondered why. "And I am the one who led Lahnni into that trap on behalf of your mother. Though, neither of us knew what Darria had planned."

"How?"

"I used our friendship from years prior to get Lahnni to agree to come and read Darria in the hope it would reveal her plans, so your mother would be able to prepare for whatever was to come. Lahnni agreed, and I left them alone. Darria drugged Lahnni and had her locked in a room." Evan stopped and looked out the window for several moments, as if lost in his memories. "I made the decision to rescue Lahnni, which would reveal who I worked for, but I no longer cared. I had done the wrong thing and needed to make it right."

"It was a difficult position to be in."

"Yes, honor, loyalty, the vows I had taken to serve, but in the end, what won out was doing the right thing. Kahlahnni is touched by the gods, her brand proves it, but it was the simple fact that Darria was looking for vengeance and would use another person to create it, and it was wrong of me to allow it. Whether it was one of the Gifted or a branded Servant."

"I understand." Harlonngraith nodded at him.

Evannderth leaned forward, his blue eyes intense. "I don't think you do, so I will speak plainly. Your mother is no different than Darria in some ways."

Harlonngraith stilled.

"Queen Anzhellika would use Kahlahnni just as Darria wanted to. Though, oddly, she never requested a personal reading, and it never dawned on me until we were here to question why. I often wonder what she was hiding."

The prince went to speak, but Evannderth waved him into silence. "Oh, Lahnni read her, but it was brief and focused on you boys. You can hide things from a Seer if you keep your mind focused on your question, but you have to understand the gift enough to do it. We didn't just come here to escape from Darria, we came to escape from your mother too. Lahnni would have been hunted to the ends of Segarris and beyond for her gifts by those two queens." Evannderth's voice was anguished.

"Then why do you help me now?" asked Harlonngraith.

"Because you are not your mother, and Lahnni says we must. Everything is finely balanced, decisions must be made, and we all have a part to play for the best outcome."

"That is why you have me wait to meet my Champion?" asked Harlonngraith, but he already knew the answer.

"Yes, the Champion is dear to me, and I will not have you take them to another land to fight for a man who is not worthy of the throne. I may not live in Segarris anymore, but what happens to its citizens has always been important to me."

"And me teaching at the dojo proves what?" Harlonngraith was curious.

"It shows me what type of man you are."

He couldn't help it, Harlonngraith had to know. "And how am I doing so far?"

"You need more patience," Evannderth said pointedly.

This made Harlonngraith laugh, but he did refrain from asking any further questions.

Evannderth went on. "I also hope to see that you understand while as King you can do as you wish, having your queen and the queen you cast aside, both fall pregnant to you may be an ego boost but it is detrimental to the succession of the throne and makes for uncertain times."

"I do not know what my father was thinking," admitted Harlonngraith. "I never met him more than a handful of times. He was always running off to fight another battle, even when he was not required. And then he died by slipping off a cliff when I was eight, having not named me as rightful heir." Harlonngraith shook his head. "I doubt I will ever understand his motives. But I can assure you of one thing."

"And what would that be?"

"The woman I take as queen will be treated with the highest regard and never cast aside if she cannot produce an heir. I will honor her, and hope as time goes on, I will come to love her." For some reason as Harlonngraith spoke about his future queen, all he could think about was a tall, quiet woman, with shining light brown hair and eyes that smiled at him.

Samarra

The structure was round, stone walled, and accessed by a staircase covered in lichen. Long lines of people moved through the moss-covered forest as they slowly made their way along winding paths that threaded through tall trees with overhanging vines. Sunlight shone through in pockets, and it was hard to tell what time of day it was. Two figures stood at the top of the huge staircase, both cloaked in dark colored clothing. A symbol was emblazoned over the opening of the stone wall. The taller of the two figures pulled his hood down to reveal a face of broad planes, full lips, and gray eyes. He was a prince and destined for greatness. The second figure reached up...

Marra was pulled away from her writing by her mother calling that dinner would be ready in five minutes. She looked up from where she sat in the recliner in the corner of the lounge room and smiled at her beautiful mother. It was just the two of them for dinner, so her mother had promised to make her favorite curry, because they both loved it, while it made Marra's father sweat and claim his insides were burning. As Evan was checking on the new instructor and having dinner with him, it gave the two women a chance to eat curries and catch up. "Great, I'll go wash up and then come and set the table."

Marra reread what she had just written and was happy with it... she had managed to describe the setting that had come to her in her dream last night. She ignored the fact she had inserted the handsome Harley as a prince into the scenario, and refused to acknowledge how much she thought about him. As Marra put her laptop on charge and hurried to the bathroom, she heard the front door open. Her dad was home. She quietly made her way down the hall and halted about halfway when her parents whispering reached her. She couldn't hear many words, but those she did made little sense. It was like many of their conversations at the moment.

"He is impatient," Evan whispered.

"Yes, I expect he would be," agreed Lahnni.

There was more mumbling that Marra didn't quite catch.

"Are you getting anything yet?" he asked.

"Just to be patient, and a long path that feels like it won't end."

What on earth did that mean? wondered Marra.

"Dinner is ready," called Lahnni, which made Marra jump and heart race for a few moments.

"Hi, Dad," she said as she made her way into the kitchen.

"How was dinner?"

"Great."

"I see you are having curry." He shuddered dramatically. This made them all laugh.

"How is my replacement settling in?" she asked as she set out two place mats.

"Good. No parent complaints or grumpy emails have come in, so that's a positive. He is good, not as good as you, but good."

"That's a lot of 'goods' in there," Marra noted.

Evan raised his blond eyebrows at her. "You're the writer, not me. I can say as many 'goods' as I wish."

"Sit and eat." Lahnni interrupted their good-natured bickering. She spoke in her native tongue as was the family practice when they were eating dinner. This way Marra was taught the language and had not lost it as she grew.

Marra and Lahnni began to eat, while Evan sat with them. There were so many things Marra wanted to ask about Harley but didn't want to give herself away. Her mother was always able to see more than Marra wished. It was like she could see into her true thoughts. Most of the time it was helpful, as Lahnni was quick to give comfort when Marra was growing up, and in her teens she was given space when needed. But on rare occasions, when Marra wanted to hide her feelings for whatever reason, she had learned the only way to do that was to not think about it or allude to anything close to the subject that was bothering her.

Specifically, she wanted to know how Harley was going with the self-defence classes. For some reason, it sparked jealousy in her. All those women flirting with him. Being coy and clever. Marra wished she wasn't so shy and could be clearer about how attracted she was to him. Instead, she had challenged him to a fight. *But you let him win,* her inner voice pointed out. *Yeah, but he doesn't know that. He's way out of your league. Hunz was very clear you were too boring to be with for more than a few months.* Her only boyfriend's parting words still hurt.

"All you do is read, write, and talk about stupid movies that are for children. Magic, and dragons, and fantasy worlds aren't real, and it's moronic to like them. And you spend too much time at that dojo, you have no time for me, and I should be your priority."

Evan interrupted her spiralling thoughts. "How's the writing coming along? Are you enjoying your time off and getting *good* words written?" Evan winked as he emphasized the word good.

Marra brightened. She always loved to talk about her writing, but tried not to bore people by bringing it up. "I had a great dream last night. Gave me some wonderful inspiration." She didn't mention she had cast Harley as the lead protagonist.

"Really?" Lahnni spoke softly. "What did you dream?"

"There was a huge round building in the middle of a forest and people were coming in droves to see what would happen inside. I haven't decided what will go on inside the building yet." Marra took a bite of her curry and considered her options of where the story might lead.

"Sounds interesting," her father answered.

"Any people in your dream?" Lahnni asked.

This made Marra hesitate. She was careful not to think of Harley. "I just saw two men standing at the top of a long staircase." She took another bite of her curry. "I did see a symbol which is similar to the one on Dad's hip"

"Well, that sounds exciting. A good starting point for an interesting fantasy novel," Evan said with interest.

"Yes," agreed Lahnni. "Tell us more."

Chapter 6

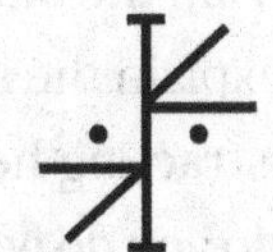

Harlongraith

The expelling whoosh of breath filled the otherwise quiet dojo. Harlonngraith grinned as he rubbed his ribs. "That will stop me from daydreaming again." He laughed.

Marra took a step back and rested on her staff. He mimicked her. He had been day-dreaming about the best way to ask her out. He had never wanted to spend time with a woman like he did with her. He found Marra fascinating.

"Don't tell me you're tired already?" she teased.

He loved it when she teased him. It was always light banter, but there was a challenge underneath that he couldn't resist. He had spent his life taming his competitive side and not rising to challenges. He had been taught to assess and only take risks when no other action could be taken. But as soon as she goaded him ever so slightly, it was enough for him to agree to her wants. "Do you have siblings?" he asked as he resumed his fighting stance and waited for her to do the same.

"No, it's always been just me." Marra stopped resting on her staff and spun it slowly before crouching into position. "What about you?"

"I have two brothers. I am the oldest. It is complicated." He didn't know how to explain the situation, so asked another question while distracting her by starting to move in a semi-circle. "What do you do when you are not here?"

"Read and write books."

"Truly?" He was taken aback.

"Yes, truly." Her voice held an edge he hadn't heard before.

He wondered what he had said wrong. Harley steered away from the conversation, even though he would have loved to know more. "Anything else?"

"I hang out with my friends."

He thought about that for a few moments. He had always longed to have friends to hang out with. His mother had kept him and his brother so isolated as children that Harley had found it near impossible to make a friend. When he had been sent to train with the Pomaikka, he had then hoped to make a friend, but while they were respectful, he was never accepted as one of them. "That must be fun." He hoped he didn't sound too wistful.

"You need to work on your feet placement." Marra completely changed topics.

"Huh?" he said, not keeping up.

She looked pointedly down at his feet, as they circled each other. "You are crossing your feet too far, if you are not careful, you won't be able to recover your footing properly if someone comes at you quickly."

Harley frowned as he fought the want to look at his feet. *Was she right? There is no reason for her to say something that wasn't true,* he reasoned. *But she could be trying to put you off guard.*

Marra rolled her lovely brown eyes at him and moved sharply, stepping forward and plunging her staff straight at his feet. She didn't swing it to hit his legs, she simply stuck the staff out. Harley's feet became entangled as he went to take another step, and with flailing arms, he fell backward, letting the staff go. She stood over him and gently tapped his chest with her staff. "Three," she said the word softly.

"You win," Harley declared. He was completely impressed with how quickly she had beaten him this time. He held out his hand.

Marra looked at his hand for several moments and Harlonngraith held his breath. Would she take it? He hoped she would, the skin-on-skin touch was something he longed for. She reached out and grasped it, stepping back and helping to haul him to his feet.

Her hand fit his perfectly. Her skin was soft, her grip tight, and confident in its ability. Harlonngraith held her hand for several seconds longer than what was appropriate, but he didn't care. He wished he could hold her hand forever.

"Would you like me to help you with your feet?" Marra offered while he continued to hold her hand. She did not pull away.

"Yes, please." Harlonngraith finally let go of her hand and went to pick up his staff.

For the next fifteen minutes, Marra guided him through where he should be stepping, explaining that with his longer legs he should be taking advantage of being able to step forward further and be inside the swing arc to halt an attack, but that he needed to keep his side movements more concise and smaller so his feet didn't get tangled. He learned quickly, and by the end of the sparring session, he had improved and Marra was no longer able to trip him.

"You are a much better instructor than me," he said admiringly as they put the staffs away and set about tidying the dojo.

"You did much better with the children today," Marra complimented him. "I think I have just had more practice than you at teaching."

"I think you are being kind."

"No, not at all."

Harlonngraith changed the subject. "Are you going out with your friends tonight?" he asked, surprised at how forward he was.

Marra turned to look at him, as she slung her backpack over her shoulder. "Not tonight. I was going home to write."

He tried not to show his disappointment. "Very well. Have a good night."

He watched her cock her head to the side, it was one of his favorite things she did. "Why do you ask?" Her words were soft.

"I don't live far from here," he started and stopped. Harlonngraith didn't want to proposition her, he wanted to spend time with Marra and get to know her. "I live alone." He tried and stopped again. He was making it worse. "Well, that came out all wrong," he finally said.

This made her laugh. "Would you like to try again?" she offered, her brown eyes sparkling at him.

He bowed to her, his courtly manners coming through. If only she understood that as the heir to the throne, and since the death of his father when he was much younger, Harlonngraith had not bowed to anyone.

Everyone bowed to him. "What I was attempting to do, but it appears was quite clumsy at, was ask if you would like to join me for dinner tonight?"

"Dinner sounds wonderful." He was relieved to hear her say that.

"Would it be appropriate to ask you to my house? Or we could go out, but I do not know what the food will be like at any of the eating places," Harlonngraith explained.

"Going to your place is fine."

He grinned at Marra but resisted the temptation to pick her up and swing her around. Instead, he put on his long trench coat to ward off the late afternoon cooling air and held out his arm to escort her out of the dojo.

She rested her hand on his forearm like she was his queen, and they moved to the door where he held it open for her and then waited patiently for her to lock it. "Okay, what are we eating?" she asked as he retook his arm.

He coughed guiltily. "There is something I must admit."

"Go on," Marra's voice had an edge to it.

"I don't know how to cook, and I have no food in my house."

Her face brightened and his heart thudded loudly.

"Would you like me to cook for you?" she asked.

"Only if you wish to."

"I would be honored to cook for you."

Harlonngraith smiled broadly and he wondered how the world didn't hear his heart beating faster just thinking about being close to Marra for the next few hours.

Chapter 7

Samarra

Marra tried not to notice Harley clinging to the door handle while she drove through the roundabout. He looked so nervous. "You don't like driving?" she asked. *Maybe he had been in an accident? Maybe his family were so poor they never had a car? Maybe you have an overactive imagination and should mind your own business,* she told herself.

"I am not used to driving. I come from a place that had more horses than cars."

"What else didn't you have?" she asked, curious.

"I honestly don't know. It's only once it is pointed out do I know that it is not something I have had before, aside from the obvious things. Like cars and phones."

"Makes sense." She stopped herself from commenting that how could he possibly not have a phone.

Marra pulled into a car park. "What about chocolate and ice-cream?"

Harley frowned and shook his head. "What are they?"

"Oh, you are in for a treat. They are delicious foods." She quickly changed her mind about what she was going to cook for him. "We are having chocolate brownies with chunks of chocolate, and vanilla ice-cream for dessert," Marra announced as she grabbed a cart and headed for the door.

"I trust you." His gray eyes looked down at her and Marra's stomach fluttered. "Are we having anything else but brownies?" he asked.

"Well…" She drew the word out, teasingly for a moment. "We are having fish."

It didn't take long for Marra to choose all the produce they would need. As she wasn't sure exactly what was at Harley's place, she also picked up a few herbs, spices, and oils. She was working under the assumption that when he said there was no food, there really was no food. Marra tried not to point out things on the shelves and ask him if he knew what it was or how to eat it. She was fascinated but worried it would seem rude or that she was making fun of him. Marra insisted on paying and did it so quickly that she was certain he didn't understand what had happened until they were headed for the door with him pushing the cart.

The drive to his place was quick, and she did her best to continue ignoring his white knuckle grip on the door handle. She pulled up to the side of the road as he directed and looked up at the two-story apartment complex. "How many units?" Marra asked as she turned the car off.

"I don't know." He shrugged.

They carried the bags of groceries into the building and Marra followed Harley up the stairs to the second floor. He fished around in his pocket to find his key and unlocked the door and flicked on the light. Marra tried not to pass judgement as she entered the living room. It was tiny, and it seemed more so with Harley's huge hulking frame standing in the middle of it. She dumped the bags she carried onto the bench and pulled out the ice-cream. "Can you please put that in the freezer?" she asked as she continued to unpack.

"Yes." He picked up the blue tub of vanilla ice-cream and opened the freezer to reveal a few boxes of frozen meals and several plastic containers, they looked similar to the ones her mother used. "Would you mind if I quickly had a shower and got changed?" he asked.

"Not at all," Marra answered. "I'll start on dinner."

Marra hummed softly to herself as she turned the oven on and opened cupboards and drawers to find all the things she needed. She noted that Harley had been telling the truth: he really did have nothing but frozen meals, but thankfully, the apartment was fully stocked with pots, pans, and utensils. As she was closing the oven door on the baking tray now filled with a fish, whole small potatoes, and asparagus, Harley walked out towel drying his hair. Marra instantly stopped humming and let the oven door slide from her hands the last few inches, and it made a thud in the now quiet kitchen. She swallowed hard around the lump in her throat and averted her eyes from his crotch. Marra had never seen Harley in anything other than his ghi and coat, and now this gorgeous man stood before her in a plain black t-shirt, with a deep v neck that revealed a small patch of chest hair, and grey sweatpants that clearly outlined what was underneath.

"How was your shower?" she attempted to sound casual as she fought to keep her eyes on his face.

"I love the constant hot water of the shower. Usually, I would have to have a bath to have the water hot for so long." He put the towel down and ran his hand through his light brown hair, giving it a shaggy appearance. "What can I do to help?"

"You can help me make the brownies while we wait for the fish to bake."

"Okay, but be warned, when I said I didn't know how to cook, I really did mean it. Like not at all. I was never allowed in the kitchens."

Marra assumed that the way he said kitchens was simply his accent and not knowing English perfectly. If she stopped to think about it, Harley was doing extremely well to teach class in another language when he had only arrived weeks before. His accent was strong but most of the words he used were a little more formal, though they were typically the correct ones. "No cooking with your Mum?" she asked.

"No, my mum was busy running everything. I was expected to learn well and be better than my peers in all areas of study."

"That is a lot of pressure," Marra commented. She thought of her own upbringing. Hers had been fairly average. Well, as average as you could expect when your mother owned a tarot reading, spiritual shop and seemed to be able to sense things when she shouldn't.

"I guess it is a lot of pressure, but I have never known any different."

Marra handed him a bowl and their fingers brushed for a moment. It was like electricity shot between them. She held her breath to gain her equilibrium again. "Here," she said softly. Harley held the bowl awkwardly and she laughed, breaking the moment. "It won't bite you."

"You sure about that?" His voice was dubious.

"I'll protect you," she teased, shocked that her shyness was nowhere to be seen.

"With you protecting me, I have nothing to worry about then." He winked, and her stomach responded with another flutter.

"Will you tell me more about your family?" she asked as she measured and handed him things to dump into the bowl, occasionally indicating that he needed to stir.

"There is not much to tell. My father died when I was eight, he was away with the army a lot."

"Did he die in a war?" she asked. Marra wanted to reach out and hug him to tell him how sorry she was, but stopped herself.

"No, he slipped off a cliff. I rarely saw him and didn't know him well."

She put her hand on his forearm and squeezed gently. "I am sorry."

"Thank you." Harley stirred the sticky chocolate mixture. "My brother is in the priesthood. When I was sent away to learn at a special school, he was sent to an Arch Deacon to complete his studies. We are close, and I don't see him as much as I would wish."

Marra took the bowl and spoon from Harley and poured the batter into a baking tin she had found. "And your other brother?" she prompted, noting that he only answered what she asked.

"Tom is my half-brother. We share the same father. I have never lived with him, and know little about him." His words were short and sharp, he was clearly not enjoying talking about himself. "You said you write," Harley said, completely changing the topic.

It was Marra's turn to feel uncomfortable. Writing was not something she brought up around strangers. Most people were truly interested, but it put her in a position where her shyness vied with her want to talk about all things writing. "Yes, I am having time off to write."

"And how is it going?"

"I have been working on something for a while, but I have recently found new inspiration, so I am working on that." She wondered how he would feel about being made her main male character. A prince, no less. Most people only like the idea in theory, as they didn't want to be seen as having any faults, and all characters had to have a fault or two.

The timer on her phone sounded. "Dinner should be ready." She arched an eyebrow at him. "Do you at least know how to set a table?" she asked.

"I know we need a knife and fork and a goblet."

Her heart swooned for some reason when he said goblet instead of wine glass. Marra was letting her imagination run wild, picturing him sitting at a large table, dominating the room with his height, strength, and charisma, all while sipping from a huge pewter goblet... the only thing that didn't fit was that she pictured him wearing the gray sweatpants at the feast. "You handle the knife, fork, goblets, and wine and I'll serve the food. Deal?" she asked.

"A fair trade," he agreed.

Samarra

"Well, what do you think of chocolate brownies and ice-cream," Marra asked as she stood to clear the plates.

Harley leaned back in his chair and groaned dramatically while rubbing his stomach. "I don't think I have eaten anything close to that magnificent before."

"I am glad you enjoyed it." She found the plug and added soap before turning the tap on. Marra turned and gave him a cheeky smile. "I'm guessing you have never washed dishes either?"

"I wash the stuff I eat off." Harley looked at her as if he was embarrassed by his answer.

Marra laughed, she couldn't help it. "You have the basics then." She turned back and turned off the tap. "I am leaving you to do the dishes. I need to get home and have a shower from our sparring session earlier." Everything in her told her to linger, but she ignored her desires and picked up her bag.

"You are really going to leave me with all the dishes?" he sounded bewildered.

"You're a big boy. You'll be fine," Marra assured him as she headed toward the front door.

"Marra?" He drew out her name. She reached for the door. Harley came up behind her and put his hand over hers. "Thank you for a perfect evening," he said as he took her hand and spun her around to face him.

She looked up into his gorgeous eyes and took in his broad forehead and sharp cheekbones, his now dry, but still shaggy light brown hair, and his perfect gray eyes that she could disappear in. Harley was everything she secretly dreamed of in a man. "Thank you for inviting me." Marra could have kicked herself. All night she had been clever and teasing, and again she had become flustered and words failed her at the worst time.

Harley gave no warning. He simply continued to hold her hand while he stepped forward and backed her up against the door. His body barely brushed hers, but Marra felt her insides heat. She didn't fight or resist the move. Her breathing was shallow as she lifted her head and found herself standing on her toes. Harley lowered his head and pressed himself against her as his lips found hers. The world around them ceased to exist as Marra joined her tongue with his as she let go of his hand to reach up to rest her hands on his shoulders. Everything was slow and soft, gentle and sweet. He kissed her over and over, his tongue darting out to meet hers before withdrawing. She groaned quietly.

Harley pulled his face away from hers and kissed the tip of her nose before stepping back completely. Marra peeled herself off the door and came back down to the heels of her feet. She reached around behind her to find the door handle again. "Thank you," she whispered, now so frazzled she had no idea what to say.

He bent down and moved his lips to her ear. "I hope it is not long until I see you again." And with those parting words, Harley reached around her again, but this time he opened the door and allowed her to leave.

Chapter 8

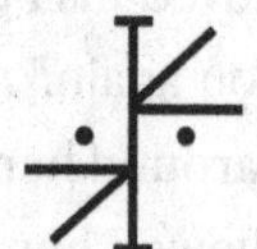

Harlonngraith

"**G**ood, very good." He removed the woman's hand from around his throat. "Just remember, ladies, if you have claws..." He held up the hand of the woman he was demonstrating with for them all to see, "make sure you use them." There was much laughter, which he didn't quite understand, but he smiled and again thought to himself how strange this world was.

The woman tossed her hair over her shoulder and simpered at him. He smiled blandly at her. While he had no idea how to handle Marra and his growing feelings for her, he could expertly decline a clear invitation from this woman. He had, of course, slept with a few women—after all he was a man with a libido—but he had been trained, and educated, and made to understand that his heart could never belong to another when his queen would be decided for him. Harlonngraith had always found it easy to abide by his mother's rule: that he give his heart to no one, as loving someone made you weak, but now he wasn't so sure.

Marra was amazing, brilliant, funny, kind, beautiful, and challenging... the list of what he loved about her was almost endless. He knew he was smitten, and he hoped she felt the same way. Harlonngraith pushed away the idea that he was here to find his Champion, not to fall in love. Maybe he could do both? Maybe he could fall in love and figure out a way to convince the chosen Champion to follow him at the same time? It was too complicated to think about, and Harlonngraith had to admit it had been a freeing two weeks of enjoying himself and not continually planning his next move for the throne. Captain Evannderth said to trust him regarding when it was time to find his Champion, and Harlonngraith, after spending time with him, chose to do just that.

He looked at the clock and did the math—five more minutes and he would be done for the day. The women's self-defense class was the only one he taught today, and as it was only mid-morning, it would give him the rest of the day to start thinking about what his next step would be. "Okay, ladies, let's do some stretches for cool down. Please, line up," he called out as he moved to the front of the mat.

The front door opened, and the entire class looked to see who it was. Harlonngraith smiled broadly as Marra came in wearing a ghi. Maybe his plans for the day have changed.

He coughed loudly to get everyone's attention, and most turned back immediately. He quickly put them through a cool down stretch, instructing them to breathe deeply and to not strain themselves, just feel resistance.

Harley was peripherally aware of Marra the whole time as she moved quietly about the room. As soon as he dismissed the class, several hurried over to her to hug her in greeting, while a few women rushed to him. A few of the women quickly thanked him or called out a greeting to Marra as they left, but there were three women who, regardless of how polite and clearly not interested he was, lingered, and brushed their hand on his arm when trying to gain his attention from the others, laughed too loudly at his jests, and their clothing had become smaller every time they came to class. They were wearing almost nothing, and it was scandalous. Bed clothing covered more. Marra had worn tight clothing when they had sparred but her bare skin had never shown around her stomach or bare legs.

"Thank you for a great class, ladies, but if you will excuse me, I wish to speak to Marra." Harlonngraith used his best court manners. He nodded his head at the women and tried not to stare at the one that looked like she had huge spider legs on her eyes.

"Hey." He tried to sound casual but his voice came out a little squeaky. Harlonngraith could feel his face grow hot, and he looked anywhere but at her as he stood awkwardly behind the women she was chatting with.

Marra looked up at him. "Hey, I have run into a nasty case of writer's block, so came down to see if you were interested in sparring to take my mind off things?"

Harlonngraith caught the wink one of the women gave her and then murmured, "Nice plan," before they said their goodbyes to both of them and headed for the door.

By now his face had returned to its normal temperature. "Sparring sounds good."

She beamed at him. "Let's wait until everyone has left. I don't feel like having an audience."

"Yes," he quickly agreed. He noticed one of the women struggling to open the door as her hands were full of clothing and bags. "Here, let me," Harlonngraith said as he hurried toward the door. He held it open for the grateful lady and then for several more as they said their thank you's and goodbyes. Two of the scantily clad women had put coats on by now and lingered a little longer at the door before finally leaving. He wanted to sigh as he closed the door but refrained; they were just like the courtiers who were searching for husbands. Forward, obnoxious, and deliberately misconstruing social cues. He locked the door so none of them could come back in and disturb them.

"How was your class?" asked Marra, but he noted an edge to her voice.

"Good. Most of them take it seriously."

"They're taking something seriously," she muttered.

Harlonngraith chose to ignore the comment. Maybe it was a cultural thing he wasn't understanding. "Do you want to spar with staffs again?" he asked.

"No." Her answer was short.

He frowned and moved to the center of the mat. "What would you like to do?" he asked.

"Punch you. Hard." Her words made him laugh, which made Marra scowl.

Had he missed something? She walked to him, retying her black belt as she did. Her ghi was black, rather than the typical white, and had light blue cuffs on both the sleeves and pant legs. "Why are you wearing black?" he asked, curious.

"You would have to ask my instructor that. He is the one who gave it to me when I reached a certain level in my training."

"Are you angry at me?" Harlonngraith asked. He wasn't enjoying her snappy answers and was not used to being spoken to in this way. He was trying to keep his own temper in check but was finding it increasingly hard when he felt he had done nothing to warrant this bluntness.

In response, she jumped, spun, and kicked, in an impressive display of athleticism, showing him the perfect round house. Harlonngraith leaped back by instinct, which was probably the only reason he didn't have a broken nose. Once he regained his footing, he swung at her head and followed it quickly with a leg sweep, which should have taken her down.

Marra blocked the punch easily and jumped, showing little effort as his leg passed under her uselessly. "I'm not one of the women in the self-defence class who you can impress that easily."

"What," was all he got out before she launched another flurry of punches and kicks at him. This time she was more focused and two connected, making him grunt.

"Marra, I don't want to hurt you," Harlonngraith warned.

"What if I push you too far, will you lose your temper and hurt me?" she spat the words. "I'd like to see you try," she challenged.

"I will never lose my temper with you. I meant I might hurt you accidentally."

"Oh, sorry," she said, but at the same time kicked him hard in the thigh. "Some of the men in class occasionally get tired of me beating them and try to harm me."

"That's disgusting," said Harlonngraith, not hiding his shock.

Marra blocked several of his counter moves before speaking. "It actually turned out to be a good thing. It sure taught me to fight like my life did depend on it. Also trained me to take a proper punch."

While she was talking, Harlonngraith was calculating his next move. He lunged for her, reaching out and grabbing her upper arms. The next thing he knew he was lying on his back and his eyesight was slightly blurry. "Ouch," he muttered.

"Sorry," she looked down at him. "Pure instinct."

He held his hand out so she could help him up, but when she offered her hand, he grasped it tightly and pulled her down beside him. She was quicker and far more agile, but he still had sheer brute strength and size on her. He swung his leg and rolled over, sitting on her stomach, a knee on each side, while grabbing both her hands and pinning them over her head. Rather than fighting, Marra stilled. "Are you going to tell me why you are being grumpy with me?"

Her gorgeous brown eyes glared at him. "No."

"But you are grumpy with me?" he tried to clarify.

"Yes," she ground the word out between clenched teeth.

"I'm not letting you go until you tell me why you are upset. It makes me sad to think I have made you sad." He had no idea what was wrong but thought maybe if he were honest about his feelings she might be about her own.

"You have not made me sad," Marra's voice was quiet. "It is nothing. I am being silly." She closed her eyes.

"Tell me, please."

Marra kept her eyes closed. "I didn't like the way a few of the women touched you."

Understanding finally dawned on him. How stupid could he have been? She was jealous. Harlonngraith lowered his head slowly, making certain he kept a tight grip on her, knowing that she most assuredly had been taught how to get away from a much larger predator who had her pinned. He gently kissed her forehead and pulled back.

Marra's eyes flew open.

"I don't like the way they touch me either," he admitted.

"You don't?"

"The only person I want touching me in any way is you." Harlonngraith watched her. He was more than a tad shocked he had confessed that.

"I was being silly."

"Being jealous is okay if you speak up and ask for reassurance rather than try to punch me," he reasoned. "I will always be happy to assure you that I find you to be the most desirable woman in any room." Where were these words coming from? He had never spoken to anyone like this.

"Can you please release me?" she asked.

Harlonngraith studied her, not completely trusting that she wouldn't lash out again, after all, while he was falling in love with her, he still didn't know her that well. "I don't know. I am fairly certain I am going to be covered in bruises tomorrow and I really don't want any more."

"Harley, please let me go," she asked again, calmly.

Half expecting Marra to attack, he did what was asked and loosened his grip on her hands. She twisted one hand and he let it go, but instead of attempting to get away, she put her hand behind his head, fisted the hair at the nape of his neck and brought his head down to meet hers. Her eyes were intense as their lips joined. She tasted sweet, and delicious, like the brownies and ice-cream she had made for him the other night.

Harlonngraith's body responded, his cock growing hard as they kissed. It started off slowly and gently but soon turned to deeper kisses with their tongues joining and his body begging for him to take control and peel her clothes off so he could kiss every inch of her. He broke the kiss. "Marra," he said roughly, barely holding on to his senses. "Everyone can see us."

He watched with mild bemusement as she turned her head to the side to confirm it was still in fact the middle of the afternoon and they were clearly able to be seen through the large dojo windows by anyone who walked by. "I am most tempted to say screw it, I don't care," she confessed.

"I don't think Evan would be happy with either of us if we continued to canoodle on the mat for everyone to see."

"Canoodle?" She giggled. "Okay, no more canoodling. Let me up."

Harlonngraith moved to allow Marra to get up and deliberately groaned loudly.

"What's wrong?" she asked, her face filled with genuine concern.

"Would you believe that I was attacked by a jealous wench and my ribs hurt?" he asked innocently, hoping he had gauged her mood right.

"Unheard of. Absolutely not possible. You are so strong and tall, how could a mere woman ever hurt you?"

"I think you could easily kill me, if you chose to," he said casually. Marra laughed as she moved to gather her things. Harlonngraith stood in the center of the mat grappling with the implications of what he had said. She could kill him, easily if she chose. Yes, he had beaten her that first time they sparred, but there was something that made him feel like the truth had been revealed. There was a dawning that perhaps Marra was indeed his Champion. But instead of feeling triumphant, Harley felt nauseous. He hoped he had it wrong.

Chapter 9

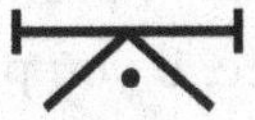

Samarra

Thinking of Harley naked, his hands and mouth on her, made Marra move quicker. She picked up her bag and shoved on her shoes, all the while secretly hoping Harley was trying to find a way to ask her to his place again. If she could do it without sounding awkward, she would invite herself.

Marra turned to find the tall, gorgeous man still standing in the middle of the mat, the look on his face made her pause before speaking. She couldn't fathom what he was thinking. If she had to guess, he looked stunned and mildly ill at the same time. His gray eyes blinked at her several times, as if not really seeing her. "Harley, you okay?" she asked, not quite sure what else to say.

"Sorry, I was just trying to decide whether to invite you back to my place for leftover brownies and ice-cream now you have threatened to kill me," he joked.

His voice was warm, friendly, but it didn't reach his eyes; instead, they looked haunted. Marra wrestled with her inner self about pushing the issue. In the end, she decided to give him space, and if he was still behaving oddly later she would try to get him to open up. Some-times we needed time to process something...she would allow him that, but Marra also hoped he understood how much she already cared for him and that she wanted to be there to support him. "I promise to behave with no more threats of violence, if you promise to talk to me if there is something wrong," she said the words softly, as she walked to him and took his hand.

Harley squeezed her hand and bent to gently kiss her forehead. "There is much to tell, but not today." He lifted her chin with his free hand until she was looking into his beautiful eyes, his face hovered so close to her own. "Today, I want to know you." He kissed her deeply, pas-sionately, his touch showing her more than words would ever do. Harley pulled back. "Would you do me the honor of coming home with me?"

Marra loved the way he spoke to her. So formal, as if he truly was a prince with all his fancy court manners. She felt like curtsying. "Yes, but this time we get Uber Eats."

"I might agree if I knew what Uber Eats was." He frowned at her as he let go of her chin.

"Oh, oops." Marra blushed as her jest now sounded silly. "You can order food from a restaurant and they bring the food to you."

Harley's face brightened and he squeezed her hand. "Yes, I have other plans for you. No cooking for me tonight."

Her blush deepened but she didn't look away. "I liked cooking for you," she insisted.

"You can cook for me anytime you wish, but not tonight." His gray eyes were intense as they studied her. He licked his lips in a slow sensuous sweep, giving her a clear indication of where his thoughts lay.

Marra almost swooned. "Fuck me," she said quietly to herself.

Harley moved to brush his lips against her ear. "That's the plan." He exhaled softly, sending a thrill along her skin.

"How quickly can we get to your place?" she teased.

He lifted the hand he still held and kissed it like a gentleman. "Would it appear unseemly if I forced you to run home?" he joked.

Marra laughed loudly, dimming the sexual tension that had been building between them. She let go of his hand, and without either of them speaking another word, they collected their belongings, locked the door, and began the short walk to Harley's. She would think about her car later.

They walked briskly and within a few minutes they were climbing the stairs to the second-floor apartment. Harley fumbled with the keys to open the door, which made Marra giggle. He looked startled for a moment, but then joined in the laughter. "I am nervous," he admitted, his voice rumbling in the way that always set her stomach to clenching and her desire aflame.

She gently took the keys from his hand and found the right one to unlock the door. Marra bowed to him, and spoke brightly. "After you." She gestured with her hand.

Harley gave her a piercing look and cupped her face with both hands. "Never bow to me. You are not subservient. You are my equal in every way."

Marra nodded her understanding, realizing as she did that if another man had uttered those words she would have laughed, but from Harley they made sense. His formality was intoxicating. He walked in and she followed, closing and locking the door behind her. She turned to find him standing closely behind her. He took up most of the hallway and she swallowed hard as he advanced on her. Marra backed up to find herself again pressed against the front door. This time there were no soft, gentle kisses. Harley devoured her, his lips pressed hard forcing hers open, his tongue questing immediately to join with her. Marra clung to him, pushing her body against his, raising herself up on her toes. He moaned deeply and her insides roared with need.

Without warning, he lifted her and she stopped kissing him, pulling her head back to look at him in wonder as she wrapped her legs around a standing man for the first time in her life. This was something she had secretly longed for, but at six-foot and well-muscled, she never thought she would find a man capable. He made it feel natural and didn't look to be struggling at all. "I need a shower." He spoke bluntly. "But I am not letting you out of my arms so you are coming with me."

Marra's insides quivered at his declaration. She kissed Harley and allowed him to carry her through the bare kitchen and into his bedroom, which was sparsely furnished with a large bed and two bedside tables. He put her gently down. "Take your shoes off," he ordered.

He removed his shoes, while Marra removed her own. His eyes never left hers. She moved to undo her black belt. "Stop," he ordered. Her hands stilled. "I will do that."

She stood there and watched him remove his own coat, untie his own black belt, and then undo the knots that held his top in place. The top hung open, but he didn't take it off; instead, he left it and moved to her. With reverence and care, he undid the black belt with its two more stripes than his own, and folded it neatly, placing it on the end of the bed. Harley then untied the two knots that held the top in place. His large, warm hands moved to her shoulders and Marra held her breath as he pushed the top from her shoulders and let it slide down her arms and to the floor, revealing a simple black sports bra. She was ever practical.

Marra moved to do the same to Harley, lifting her hands to his shoulders but only made it halfway when he gasped in clear shock. "What?" she asked, concerned with his odd reaction.

Harley grabbed both her lower arms and turned them over, revealing a tattoo on each inner wrist. "These."

Marra frowned. "You don't like tattoos?" she asked, confused.

"Who are you?" he asked, his voice demanding, but less sensual and far more authoritative.

"What do you mean?" Marra straightened herself and held her head high.

"Give me your full name," Harley's voice was the lowest rumble she had heard from him.

"Samarra Kahlahnni Cellecia Durrand," she spoke the name proudly.

Marra didn't know what to expect from Harley's strange behavior but it wasn't him falling to his knees in front of her. "What are you doing?" she asked, alarmed.

"Honoring you. These markings represent my people. I did not expect to find them here and on you."

"These are the symbols my parents carry. I did it to honor them."

"This." He dropped her left hand and took her right in both his hands. "This represents your father. Evannderth Durrand, a great soldier, and an even greater man. This brand is for warriors." He leaned forward and pressed his lips to her tattoo.

Marra blinked rapidly. What was happening? It seemed surreal, and yet appropriate. Her feelings of deja vu were growing, but instead of bothering her, the world felt like it was finally settling her into her rightful place.

Harley let go of her right wrist and held out his hands, without knowing why she held out her left arm, wrist upwards. His voice was hushed when he spoke. "This represents your mother, Kahlahnni. It is a symbol that shows you are touched by the Gods. She is the only one to wear it in three generations." Harley kissed the tattoo, his lips pressed against her pulse for several seconds and her feelings of deja vu exploded. The bedroom dropped away and she stood on a dais, clad in a silver and pale blue armoured bodice with a flowing skirt that was the color of her favorite blades. Harley still knelt before her, kissing her wrist, but now he wore a large ermine robe and a crown. Marra shook her head, her imagination obviously running wild. The vision disappeared and she was once again standing in Harley's bedroom.

Slowly, he moved his lips from her wrist and kissed her with soft butterfly kisses up to her inner elbow and then up to her shoulder, coming to stand before her as he did. Once her arms were free, she did what she had been wanting to do since the moment she had walked into the dojo that first day her friends had convinced her to check out the new instructor. Marra reached up and repeated what Harley had just done to her. She pushed his top from his shoulders but trailed her hands down his chest as the fabric fell away. In her opinion, he was perfect. A stunning sculptured Greek God, Apollo came to mind. Towering, chiselled beauty. Marra ran her hand through his lightly curled chest hair before continuing over his hard, defined abs. She trailed her fingertips along the top of his pants as she leaned forward and took his nipple into her mouth. Marra swirled her tongue around the hard tip before biting it and sucking. She rubbed her hand over the front of his pants, feeling him harden, straining to be set free.

"Shower," he growled at her as he stepped back and tugged his pants down, over his hips, allowing them to fall to the floor and display a perfect, hard cock in proportion to the rest of the huge man.

It was Marra's turn to lick her lips. She grinned as she pulled her sports bra over her head and dropped it on the floor, and soon her pants and briefs joined his. They both stood there, naked. Strong, elongated limbs defined with exceptional muscle tone. She had never felt more in connection with someone.

Marra followed him into the bathroom and waited for him to turn on the shower. She looked at the small glass cubicle—it was going to be a tight fit. She noted that the glass panels went all the way to the ceiling, which was fortunate for Harley, or the bathroom would be soaked every time he showered. Marra admired his back muscles as he stepped into the shower, and she imagined sliding her oiled hands over them.

"Samarra?" He said her name, jarring her out of her daydream. No one called her that.

"Why did you call me that? Everyone calls me Marra." She moved into the shower with him. The warm water was welcoming.

Harley held up his hand and indicated he wanted her to turn around. "I am not everyone. I like Samarra."

"It is very formal," she answered as she turned like instructed and faced the now closed door.

"If you haven't noticed, I like formal." His voice was mild.

"Yes, I like it, most of the time. But..." She stopped as he pulled gently on her hair, bringing her head back, exposing her throat.

"Oh, have no fear, there is more to me than formal gestures and words." And with that said, he lowered his head and bit her neck, not enough to make a mark, but enough to have her gasp in pleasure and shock. The hand that didn't hold her hair slid over her torso, a cake of soap leaving bubbles in its wake. While Harley continued to bite, suck, and lick her neck, his hand washed her. Over her high breasts, across her own ab-defined stomach, around to her arse, and up her back to cross over her shoulders. She moaned loudly as he dropped the soap and now skimmed his soapy hand down her body and over her mound and into her folds. Instinctively, she changed her stance, allowing him better access. Marra leaned into him as he washed her. He let go of her hair and brought his arm around to circle her body just below her bust, pulling her into his chest and holding her up as his fingers pushed into her while the base of his palm pressed firmly on her clit, moving in a slow circular motion. She rested her head against his chest and surrendered to the feelings he created in her.

Marra's breathing grew heavier and she made a high-pitched sound from the back of her throat. She had never done that before.

"I want to hear you make that sound forever." He spoke the words into the top of her head.

His words made her repeat the sound and as his hands moved over her and in her, Marra's moans grew louder, almost demanding in their need to be released. Her legs began to shake as her orgasm grew, she teetered on the edge trying to hold onto the sublime feeling where you hang in between the moment of pure physical bliss and being too sensitive to touch. Her body shattered and fell into the abyss calling out Harley's name twice as she contracted around his fingers and he held her up.

Samarra

"You know what?" she asked, arching an eyebrow at him as she closed the curtains against the fading light of the afternoon. The room was still light enough to see, but in her opinion a little more sensual.

"What?" he asked as he sat on the end of the bed, towel-drying his hair.

"I love your commanding ways, but I think you need to learn to take orders too. I get the feeling you are always in control." She drew the words out slowly as she deliberately dropped her towel and stalked toward him.

Harley stopped drying his hair and looked at her suspiciously. "What do you have in mind?"

"I want you to give up control to me." Marra stopped in front of him, planting her feet a little apart and placing her hands on her hips. She hoped she looked as confident as she felt in this moment.

She watched him swallow hard. "I let you beat me up today already, isn't that giving up enough control?" he asked.

"Let?" She raised her voice.

"Well, okay. I didn't *let* you beat me up," he amended. "Bad choice of words." He reached out and ran his finger from the hollow at the bottom of her throat, between her breasts, over her belly button and it came to rest at the top of her trimmed pubic hair. "I like being in control. Don't you like it when I tell you what to do?"

"I like it very much. In the bedroom." She made it clear. "But I also like knowing you trust me."

"Damn it, Samarra."

"What?"

"Well, when you put it like that, how can I say no?"

Marra grinned. "Hold out your hands, wrists crossed," she told him. Marra held her breath. Would he really do what she requested? Did he trust her?

Slowly, he raised his arms and held them out to her, wrists crossed. Marra stepped beside him and picked up the neatly-folded black belt he had laid there when he undressed her earlier. Before she could second guess her choice, Marra wrapped the stiff fabric around his wrists, it wasn't the ideal material, but it would do. She knotted the belt twice before gathering the ends and tugging on them while stepping backwards, forcing Harley to stand.

He did not look amused but did not resist. She grinned at him as she spoke. "I think we need to make sure you are dry." Marra unwrapped the towel from his hips and began to slowly rub in soft circles across his shoulders before moving down one arm and coming up again, then crossing over and doing the other arm. After that, she moved on to the broad expanse of chest and the gorgeous curly hair. She took her time over his stomach before moving around him to thoroughly dry his perfectly sculptured back and arse. Marra then did the back of each leg before moving around to the front. Finally, her towel made it to his balls where she gently cupped them in her hand, and smiling up at him, squeezed until his eyes widened. She stopped and when he relaxed, she squeezed again. This made him pant. "You good?" she asked as she squeezed for a third time.

Harley's breath came out ragged as he brought his arms down over her and encircled her. She let his balls go and dropped the towel as Harley kissed her fervently. Marra surrendered to the kiss and melted into his tied embrace. Her heart pounded, and blood rushed in her ears as her lust and want grew. By this point, Marra could think of nothing but the idea of having him inside her. She was on the pill so had no concerns for falling pregnant, but she had a fleeting thought that someone this handsome must have had many partners. Marra kicked herself for not thinking about having this conversation before they were here, and it would kill the mood and be awkward doing it now. "Harley?" she said softly against his lips, not wanting to break the moment but knowing she couldn't put it off.

"Yes?" he looked at Marra as if he was ready to worship her. "I will do anything you ask of me if you will be mine?"

Marra blinked up at him for several moments. "We need to talk about protection first. Do you have any or have you been tested? Are you safe?" He was only her second partner, and she did not know how to broach the subject delicately or cleverly so blurted it all out.

Harley stilled and looked down at her. "I am sorry, but I do not understand the questions. Safe? Protection?"

"I am on the pill, so no fear of getting pregnant, and have been tested, no disease here," she admitted.

"I have no diseases, if that is what you're asking. It has been a while for me too. My life is complicated and finding a bed partner is not high on my list."

"Oh." Marra's heart sank.

"Samarra, I do not wish for just a bed partner, I want more. I want connection, I didn't understand that until I met you." Harley kissed her gently. "I asked you to be mine, remember? But you did not answer."

A weight lifted off Marra's heart and she smiled at him as her worries eased. With the difficult conversation had, now it was time to see just how well they fit together. The heat between her legs rose and she kissed him, hard. "Let's see how well you do before I answer your question," she teased, though in her heart her answer was she would be his forever if he should just ask.

"What would you have me do, my queen?" His words were cheeky, but his eyes said he was serious. She liked how he had skipped the pretty princess title and had gone straight to queen.

"Lay down on your back and raise your arms over your head," Marra ordered.

Harley did what he was told, raising his bound wrists over her, before sitting on the bed and wriggling up until he lay down and raised his hands over his head.

"What a well-trained soldier you are," she purred at him. He was magnificent to look at. Marra wasted no time on extended foreplay—that would happen another time. Instead, she knelt onto the bed and crawled up in between his legs, ducking her head to run her tongue along the full length of his hard cock. Harley moaned in pleasure, and Marra watched him strain against the belt as she took hold of him and rubbed her thumb over the top of his cock, spreading his precum before pumping her hand up and down several times, marveling at his size.

Marra moved to straddle Harley and rubbed herself against him, making both of them begin to breathe heavier. She leaned forward and kissed him while she moved her hips to have him resting against her entrance. Ever so slowly, Marra rocked her hips as Harley raised his. It was delicious to feel herself stretching to accommodate him. Another of her high-pitched moans escaped as she began to heavily rock against him, her clit rubbing against his pubic bone combining with the deep penetration was incredible.

Harley strained his arms against his binding and Marra moved one of her hands up to wrap the end of the belt around her hand to hold his wrists in place. She rolled her hips again and again, rubbing against him. The moment was perfect. For the first time, everything was in alignment, and she could feel her orgasm rushing toward her. "Oh, Harley," she whispered his name. "Don't stop," she almost begged. Marra continued to ride his gloriously large, hard cock, her clit hitting right, and with one final thrust her body stilled before convulsing with waves of pleasure for several moments.

"Let me out," he begged as Marra lay on top of him, her breathing labored. She didn't answer but unwound her hand and loosened the knot enough for him to break free. Harley's hands moved fast, one wound its way into her hair, while the other went to her hip. He slowly raised his hips and pushed into her, then withdrew, before pushing into her again.

Marra kissed him, while she raised herself just enough to create a hint of space between them—it was all she could bear to be apart from the skin-on-skin contact.

Harley continued to move, in and out, holding her in place by hair and hip. He broke the kiss and whispered, "Look at me. See me."

Marra felt her heart pound as she watched his face change as he stilled while he pumped his seed into her. She flexed her internal muscles with him, making him groan harder. "I see you," she answered him.

He let her hip go and brought his hand up to caress her face. "Be mine?"

"Yes."

Chapter 10

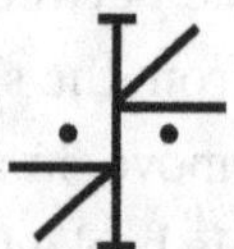

Harlonngraith

The next two weeks had been filled with teaching, which Harlonngraith was happy to say with Samarra's continued help he had begun to feel more confident with. Sparring with Samarra, with all the different weapons she had been trained to use by her father, and endless hours lying in bed asking her as many questions as he could think of to learn about her. When she asked him questions about his own life, he was either vague or distracted her with sex. It was a perfect tactic as he couldn't get enough of her.

Samarra was soon consuming his every waking thought, and if he stopped to think about it, he knew the outcome he hoped for was impossible. Harlonngraith shoved the reason as to why he was here far away from his mind. The idea of asking Samarra to be his Champion was something he now wrestled with constantly. How could he ask her to step into the Arena and fight for him and a country she has never known and either take someone's life or give up her own? It was unimaginable how only a month ago he had thought it would be simple to arrive in this foreign place and believe he had the right to ask someone to sacrifice so much for him. The arrogance now made him shudder.

"Your foot work has improved greatly," Evannderth spoke, as he returned the staffs they had been sparring with to the rack.

"Thank you, we have been working on it." The words were out before Harlonngraith had time to stop and think. He picked up his water bottle and looked out the window, pretending to be nonchalant.

He was greeted with laughter—warm, light laughter—much like his daughter's. Harlonngraith turned to face the captain.

"She just couldn't stay away, could she?"

"Sir?" Harlonngraith was confused.

"How long until she turned up to check you out?" Evan asked.

"The first Saturday I worked," Harlonngraith answered truthfully.

"Did she tell you who she was?"

"No. At first, I thought she was a parent, but the second time she came the kids told me who she was. It took another week before she told me her full name which exposed her parentage. By then, I had a strong suspicion that she was what I had been searching for."

"So, you figured it out without me?"

"Was I supposed to?" Harlonngraith wasn't sure by the tone of Evan's voice.

"I was told to allow the connection to grow naturally. I was hoping Marra might stay away and have that month of peace before we turned her world upside down. It seems fate had other ideas—or Marra did."

Harlonngraith began to ask who had told him to allow the connection to grow, but stopped himself. Obviously, it would have been Kahlahnni. He hesitated for a moment before he said what he had been worrying about. "I know it's her, she is my Champion, but are you sure she is ready?" Harley was concerned.

"Why do you say that?"

"When we first met, she challenged me. We used staffs and I won," he explained.

Evan looked surprised for a moment before a sly smile played across his lips.

"What?" Harley asked suspiciously.

"Have you ever beaten her again?" Evan asked.

"Well, no," he admitted.

"Even come close?" Evan pushed.

Harley thought back to any time they sparred. "I thought I had, but now you are putting doubts in my head."

Evannderth laughed. "She let you win that first time."

Harlonngraith frowned and went through their first fight in his head. There had been a moment when they were locked together. Their staffs connected and he had tipped it slightly to touch her neck but now he considered it, they had stood there staring at each other, but she had not moved in any way, she was good enough to have sensed his staff moving and even then she had not done anything. "She was testing me?" he said it aloud.

"That would be my guess," her father smiled.

"But, why?"

"Prince Harlonngraith, why would you think it necessary to test an opponent?"

He stopped before he blurted out the first thing that came to mind. Harlonngraith had no desire to look like a fool in front of the captain. "She wanted to see what I would do. We both had the chance to win, but she let me choose whether to retreat and continue to fight or take the win with a simple movement."

Evannderth nodded. "Yes, but it would have been more than that."

Harlonngraith walked around the edge of the mat, contemplating what he now knew about Samarra. "She wanted to see how I would react to winning. Men tend to gloat, I have noticed, and I bet she has had her fair share of gloaters over the years."

"Until she was good enough to beat them all, yes," Evan confirmed. "Did you gloat?"

"No, I complimented her on her fighting skills." Harlonngraith began to laugh. "The next time we sparred and used staffs, she told me my footwork needed work. I was skeptical, so she tripped me." True understanding dawned on him. "Samarra could have done that the first time we fought, and she chose not to." He smiled at Evan. "She is exceptional."

"No." Evan's voice was serious. "She is lethal. I trained her in ways I have never trained another. I am not sure even Lahnni knows what I created." He looked sadly at Harlonngraith. "My beautiful, precious daughter has all the skill in the world, but I will admit I do not know if she is truly capable of taking another's life. It is not something you can teach or train."

This pulled at Harlonngraith's heart. He didn't want to turn anyone into a killer, especially Samarra, but he had no choice. There was so much a stake. He felt an emptiness in his stomach and a wave of fear at her dying for him, the only thing that made the thought remotely bearable was that if she died, he would join her in death soon after, and he need not live with the loss of her. For a fleeting second, the idea of staying here forever and growing old with Samarra and just letting his half-brother take the throne was overwhelmingly appealing. But the words of his mother, constantly reminding him that it was his duty as the first born to lead the country, to find ways to stop the marauders who ransacked the Islands of Lobbegrath every other decade and to bring peace to Segarris played in his mind. Perhaps his brother Tommofey was capable of doing those things, too? When he had ever had doubts regarding this, his mother had always told him the story of her first meeting with the Seer and what she had said. *If Tommofey takes the throne there will be darkness and things will continue the way they are. If Harlonngraith takes the throne, there will be clarity; things that have been hidden for too long will be revealed.*

"She could always refuse," Harlonngraith said quietly. It was something he hadn't considered until that moment. "Samarra is strong-willed and clearly able to make her own choices. Perhaps she will not agree to aid me." He looked to Evan to see the face of a father filled with concern.

"The love I have for my daughter is endless and never to be underestimated, but I also have duty and honor to who I am. I think it is time you knew the whole truth to why we left Segarris. It is time for you to meet my wife."

Chapter 11

Samarra

Marra paced around the small pond in her family's contemplation glade. There was a feeling of on-coming dread filling her and she had no way to dispel it. Her parents' whispered conversations were becoming more frequent and her sleep more restless. She should be blissfully happy; she was falling in love with a man who wasn't intimidated by her abilities, rather he revelled in them. He was easy to talk to, always interested in her ideas, opinions, and her passions. He was a generous lover, but something had been bothering Marra since the night she had first slept with Harley and he kissed her tattoos. Why had he reacted so strongly? She hadn't thought about it at the time, clearly carried away with the moment, but now she had time to reflect, she had questions. Why didn't he have tattoos if her parents do and everyone else does? Isn't it something that must occur in between your eighteenth and nineteenth year?

The weight of the blades she carried in her hand brought her odd comfort—they always had. Out of all the weapons she had trained with, the stunning blue blades were her favorite. They fit her hand when she was ten and they still fit perfectly at twenty-one. She had been working off her tension all afternoon. Throwing the pair of blades at the target her father had made years prior, retrieving them and doing a lap of the pond before coming back and repeating the process. This had always worked in the past to get her feelings out and under control, but not today. The tension in her body was increasing, if anything.

Marra noted there were footsteps approaching as she reached her mark on the ground and threw the knife. It made a satisfying thud as it hit the center of the target. In quick succession, Marra threw the second knife with her non-dominant hand and it landed slightly to the left of its matching brother. She frowned. Her throwing was off. Usually, she could get them to slide next to each other.

There was an appreciative whistle and someone clapped slowly. "Is there anything you can't do?" he asked.

The sound of Harley's voice in the private glade of her family home made her spin. Marra didn't know what to do first. Launch herself at him and kiss him, or ask why he was here. In the end, she did both. "Why? How?" Marra explained ineloquently as she closed the gap between them quickly and jumped into his arms. She kissed him deeply, her anger forgotten for the moment as her desire for him rose to a roaring need immediately. The intensity of her emotions should have scared her, but they didn't. She would do anything for this man.

He broke the kiss but continued to hold her. "Your dad invited me." Harley grazed his thumb along her jawline.

"He knows we have met and have been sparring, but he knows nothing about our personal relationship."

"Was he grumpy that I didn't stay away?" she asked, tilting her head to the side and looking up into his beautiful face.

"Actually, he was sad that you didn't take the time to write, but also not surprised."

Marra felt instantly bad for several moments. She let go of Harley and walked over to the large, padded target to retrieve her daggers. Slowly she made her way around the pond, her desire ebbing, her uneasiness returning, she was tired of his secrets. She had no idea why it was bothering her so much today, but she hoped being more forthright would help ease her emotions.

"Can I see those knives?" he asked, holding out his hand as she walked back to him.

Marra flicked the blade into the air and expertly caught the tip without cutting herself and offered him the dagger, handle first. Harley took it and held it up to the weak sunlight of the late Sunday afternoon. Marra had always loved the way the light made the wavy blue pattern of the metal seem to undulate. "It's Damascus steel," she explained.

"No, it's not."

"I beg your pardon?"

"It is from my homeland."

"What do you mean?" She pursued the topic even though she knew what his next response would be. She had started to notice a pattern. If she asked a question he didn't want to answer, he would deflect by asking her a different question or completely derail the conversation by kissing her, which led to other things, and the question being forgotten. Well, not this time.

"I meant exactly what I said. It comes from my homeland." He frowned before his face cleared. "I am looking forward to meeting your mother."

Marra ignored the comment. She plucked the knife back from his hands. "Let's play a game," she repeated.

"I'm listening," he replied. "Games can be fun." He leered at her.

"I need knife practice so let's make it interesting. Every time I hit the bullseye you have to answer a question honestly." Marra glared at him. "No evasive answers."

"And if you miss?" he asked

"If I miss, you get to choose your prize."

His gray eyes narrowed as he studied her. "Deal, but..." He held up his hand to forestall her. "You have to throw with your left hand."

Marra smiled innocently, and threw the blade, hitting the bullseye. Wanting to start with something simple she asked, "Where are you from?"

"The Realm of Segarris."

Her eyes narrowed, what was he playing at? He knew that she would know the answer to that. Why wasn't he taking her seriously. Marra threw the second blade, this time it did what she had intended and it slid down the shaft of the first. "Why, if everyone gets a marking after their eighteenth birthday, do you not have one?"

"My brand is yet to be determined. I will either get a special one or die."

Her frustration grew further. Maybe she had misjudged him. Maybe he didn't care for her how she cared for him. Her heart broke a little and her anger came to the fore. She had always had a temper, but her discipline from her martial arts training tended to keep it in check. His refusal to answer her questions honestly was pushing her to her limits. Marra stomped over to retrieve the two blades. She spun around and demanded. "Your greatest dream?"

Harley straightened and bowed formally to her. "I am Prince Harlonngraith and I dream of being King."

Something exploded inside her as her anger welled and burst. Was it her heart breaking as he continued to mock her with stupid answers? Before she knew it the beautiful blue dagger had left her hand and hit the tree behind him sinking into the trunk.

"Why?" she cried at him, all her emotions coming at once. "Why? If you don't want to be with me, just say it. Why make up such bullshit? Was it all a game to you?" Understanding hit her. "You are here to say goodbye before you go back. It has been a month, and you were only here for a month."

"I am not lying," he whispered.

"Seriously? What kind of idiot do you think I am? Just because I read and write fantasy doesn't mean I'm going to believe some guy if he turns up and says I want to be king of the realm of such and such. There are no realms on Earth." She was hysterical. She tried to get her breathing under control. It was like a horrible joke. He had taken her most treasured things and was taunting her with them. "How very cruel you are. All you had to say was that it was time to leave, that you had a wonderful time, and were sorry to have to go. Why can't you be honest with me? What was the point of it all?" Marra was furious, she turned to flee only to find her mother and father standing at the entrance to the glade, blocking her exit.

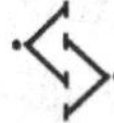

Harlonngraith

The stinging of his arm warred with the horror he felt as he watched the woman he loved unravel in front of him. He wanted to run to her, to comfort her, to tell her it was a lie, that he was trying to be funny and it had backfired, that he loved her and wanted to stay with her forever. But sadly, that would be the lie. It was time she knew the truth and he had come to not only meet Kahlahnni but to tell Samarra everything, he had just not thought through how. Now he had made an absolute mess of it. The woman he worshipped stood sobbing in the middle of this beautiful private garden after having lost complete control of her temper and had thrown a knife at him.

Harlonngraith went to move but was halted by the appearance of Evannderth and a short, dark-haired woman with a warmer skin tone and piercing deep brown eyes, just like Samarra's. This was clearly the Seer of the Pomaikka, Kahlahnni. She hurried to her daughter, and while much shorter than Marra, managed to gather her into her arms and hold her while she sobbed.

Evan walked to where Harley stood and asked quietly, "What happened?"

"I told her who I was. I have been avoiding questions for weeks. I had no idea how angry she would get."

Evan studied him long enough to make Harley start to feel uncomfortable. "How long have you two been together?" Evan eventually asked.

"Two sennights."

"Have you ever been in love?"

Harley hesitated. He tried to keep his thinking straight. His arm was truly beginning to hurt, but all he longed to do was go to Samarra and comfort her. Now, he needed to answer questions from a man he highly respected but was here to take his daughter to another world to fight and possibly die for him. Harlonngraith's stress levels were rising, and he started to do what he had been taught by the Pomaikka. He drew in a breath and focused just on that for a few seconds before releasing it. The next breath he drew in, he brought to mind the question he had been asked, blocking out everything else. It was a skill he needed to employ as the prince and would be required further when Samarra won him his crown and became king. "I was warned against falling in love by my mother. It would cause unnecessary complications and bring difficulties as I may consider their feelings, wants, and needs, and put them above my own, and as king I could not afford to do that."

He looked over at Samarra. "I always avoided an intimate connection, but with her I couldn't help it." Harlonngraith blinked and looked away. His arm really hurt. He brought his hand up to massage his bicep and winced as he touched it. Harlonngraith took his hand away to discover it was covered in blood. His dark shirtsleeve was blood-soaked and as he looked down, he noted a trail of blood coming out of the cuff over his hand and dripping into the grass.

"You're injured? How did that happen?" Evan asked, his face full of concern.

"I threw a knife at him," Marra said softly as she walked toward them, she held tight to her mother's hand.

"You what?" Evan sounded astounded. "You have been trained better than that."

"Evan, not now," Lahnni warned.

"It's fine. I deserved it. From Samarra's perspective I was playing with her emotions." Harlonngraith tried to appease everyone.

"Take off your shirt, and let me see your arm," commanded Evan in a tone that Harlonngraith immediately obeyed.

He undid his shirt one-handed and brought the shoulder down far enough to expose a large gash across the side of his bicep. This made Samarra cry out and let go of her mother's hand and rush to him. "I am sorry. I only meant to nick you, never to do this much damage."

"It's only a nick. I just bleed a lot," Harlonngraith lied, trying to make her feel better.

Her lip began to tremble as she looked at him. He wished there was a way he could take her pain and pretend this was all a misunderstanding. The worst bit was still to come. She still didn't know why he was here, who her parents were and what her role in all of this was. "Mother said what you told me is true." Her voice shook.

"Yes. I have never lied to you. I have not always told you the whole truth, but I never lied." He wanted her to understand how important it was for her to know that. "Nothing I ever tell you, no matter how hard it is to say or hear, will be a lie."

"What do you mean by that?" she asked suspiciously.

Harlonngraith looked to Evan and Lahnni for support. It was Kahlahnni that came to his rescue. "I think we should go inside. Your father needs to clean up the wound, possibly stitch it, and you need to hear the truth. All of it."

"Good idea," Evan agreed. "This way," he said to Harlonngraith.

The prince followed the man out of the secluded garden and across a loose stoned wide pathway that was lined with huge trees like he had never seen before, and back into the house Harley had walked through earlier after Evan had picked him up from home and brought him here. He held his hand up and covered his bleeding arm with his other hand, hoping to not drop blood anywhere. He was escorted to the kitchen, which had huge clear windows that overlooked a large grass covered valley.

The kitchen reminded him of home more than anything else he had seen in this strange world. Everything in the kitchen was made of dark wood or slate gray squared stone. The smell of cooking meat greeted him and his mouth began to water. He was instantly home sick.

"Sit," Evan ordered.

Harlonngraith obeyed and watched cautiously as Lahnni led Samarra in and indicated she was to sit at the table with him. The Seer then went to a cupboard and began to fill a bowl with water. Evan was opening another cupboard and brought out a clear box filled with odd things. No one spoke.

Finally, the bowl was full and Lahnni brought it to the table. Evan now began washing his hands. "Allow me to cleanse it for you," the Seer spoke softly.

"I could not ask that of you," Harlonngraith objected.

"Pfft," was her response. "I won't trip over your title, and you don't trip over mine. Agreed?"

This eased his concerns in many ways. It appeared that neither of them were angry at him for hurting their daughter.

"What are you two talking about?" Samarra interjected. "And I will clean him," she declared as she stood, towering over her mother. "I inflicted the wound, I will take care of it." She held out her hand for the cloth.

Lahnni raised an eyebrow at her but handed over the wet cloth. Harlonngraith chose not to say anything. "Mum, could you please get a towel?"

"Of course. I should have thought of that."

Samarra placed the cloth back in the bowl and turned to face him. Harlonngraith's heart constricted as he saw the pain he had caused clearly etched on her face. "Harley, I need to take your shirt off so I can clean up all the blood," she explained, her voice small.

He nodded, not sure if any words would help at this time. He lifted his arm as instructed as she slowly removed his shirt. Kahlahnni came in carrying a towel and handed it to her daughter. While Samarra laid the towel out over his leg and the back of the chair, Harlonngraith focused on the Seer. He gritted his teeth as Samarra lay the warm, wet cloth over his wound.

"Be careful of mother," Samarra warned without rancor. "I am sure some days she has the ability to read minds." The words were said in jest Harlonngraith knew, no one moved, but Samarra, who was completely oblivious. She looked up from tending his arm. "What?" she asked, clearly bewildered by the sudden shift in the kitchen.

Harlonngraith put his clean hand over hers. "Maybe you should leave that to your dad and sit down?"

Samarra shook off his hand and took several steps away from all of them. "You are all freaking me out. First, you say you're a prince, and now, you imply my mother can read minds."

"Well, not minds," Kahlahnni spoke quietly. "And I can't do it well here. Segarris is where my abilities are strongest."

Harlonngraith watched Samarra blink rapidly. He sat perched on his chair, ready to go after her if she bolted.

She didn't run, what she did was laugh. She laughed until it began to border on the edge of hysterical. Without thinking of his arm or the blood, Harlonngraith went to her. He picked her up and carried her like a baby back to his chair where he sat with Samarra in his lap. "You are not going mad, it's just a lot to take in. Do what you teach the kids when they get upset. Breathe in and hold, then let it out," he spoke to her softly, his whole world became about her. "I am going to talk, and you are going to breathe, okay?" he asked.

Samarra deliberately took a deep breath in.

"Good." He lifted his hand and brushed the hair out of her face. "I am Prince Harlonngraith, first born son to King Tommofey and Queen Anzellikah of Segarris. My father was married to Darria for many years prior to marrying my mother, but Darria was barren and never provided him with an heir. Though he loved her, he eventually cast Darria aside and married my mother, Darria's sister."

That brought out a gasp of shock from Samarra.

"Yes, I know. It didn't sit well for some, but the king has to abide by the laws of the land, and he was expected to have children with a woman of noble birth from a certain province—it is part of the accords. Every monarch must marry from a province already set out in the treaty. My father had already spent many years getting to know his wife's sister and thought of her fondly, so rather than offend a high-placed family, he simply cast aside one member and married another. Within a few years I was born and then my brother followed. What no one knew was that my father and the cast-off queen were secretly still sleeping together, and a year after my brother was born my half-brother Tommofey arrived. I was three." He stopped and looked at her. Her breathing had returned to normal. "You following all this so far?" he asked.

Samarra nodded.

"Good." Harlonngraith moved her onto his lap, so she was resting more against his shoulder. He kept looking her in the eye as he held out his arm slightly so Evan could clean it and stitch it while they talked. "Now, this may get complicated. Let me get through it and then I will answer any of your questions. Okay?"

She nodded.

"There has not been a dispute for the throne for many centuries. The first born, regardless of gender, rules and must marry someone of noble birth from an already designated region. But many generations passed when there was chaos and war, and everyone thought they had the right to rule, the priests came up with a set of instructions that had to be followed and whoever came out the victor earned the right to sit the throne of Segarris. The nobles were quick to agree in the hope it would stop warring siblings and halt the massive bloodshed as faction fought against faction."

"Your brother is challenging you for the right to rule?" Samarra sat up, a look of horror on her face.

"Yes. His mother has raised him to believe he is the rightful heir as she was the first queen."

"And people believe that?" she asked.

"People are always willing to think that someone else will give them what they want when they are not happy with their lot. Nobles are promised more land, titles, servants. Merchants are promised a change in their fortunes. Everything is politics. The general public don't care who rules as long as they have food, shelter, and no wars that take their men. They turn up to parades and bow when required, but they just want peace and not to worry about where their children's next meal is coming from."

Samarra smiled shyly at him.

"What?" he asked, suspiciously.

"You sound like a prince."

This broke the tension in the room, and everyone laughed.

"It also makes sense as to why you are incapable of taking care of yourself."

Harlonngraith had the good grace to blush. "Hey, I can wash dishes now," he protested.

This brought more laughter, but soon the mood changed as reality once again set in. Samarra asked the question he had been dreading. "So, let's skip over how you got here, I am not sure I am ready for that yet, and explain to me why you are here, rather than preparing for the right to rule ceremony or whatever it is?"

"The priest's instructions are precise and clear, and sanctioned by the gods. I should have, by rights, ascended the throne when I reached my maturity at eighteen and received my brand like everyone else. But instead, my branding ceremony was interrupted by my half-brother standing before the Arch Deacon Zussya announcing he planned on claiming his right to rule when he reached his majority, and that the ceremony could not continue as stated by the laws of the land. Nothing like a fifteen-year-old risking his life and your own for the ego of a cast off queen. A year younger and he would not have been deemed old enough to issue that challenge." Harlonngraith tried to keep the frustration from his voice.

He took a moment to look over as Evan began to sew up his arm. He winced as the needle pricked his skin, but he had suffered far worse pain. He went on to distract himself. "Tom has now reached his age of branding and has formally declared his wish to follow through on his challenge. The two of us are now known as the Challengers and must arrive at the Challenger's Arena exactly six months from the day of issue, where there will be a one-on-one fight to the death to determine the rightful ruler."

"You have to kill your brother to win the throne?" Samarra gasped.

"No. We have six months between the issuing of the challenge and the actual event as we must find someone to fight for us. This person is known as our Champion. Our Champion will be the one to face combat for us. The two Challengers and the two Champions will walk into the Arena at the predetermined date and time, but only one Challenger and Champion will exit."

"That's why you said you will either receive your special brand or die?" She sat up quickly in his lap, causing him to move his arm.

"Easy, Faffia," Evan warned his daughter as he cut the thread.

"How can you all be so calm about this?" she asked.

"We have had a long time to process this," her mother answered. "Come sit by me, and give Harlonngraith's lap a rest."

Samarra blushed as she stood up and sat between her mother and the prince. Her mother clasped Samarra's hand and didn't let go, she nodded at Harlonngraith to continue.

"Yes, to answer your question. I will receive the monarch brand after the Challenge if my Champion wins, but if my Champion is vanquished, I will be put to death."

"But why are you here?" Samarra looked confused.

"Because I received a message from the Seer of the Pomaikka that my Champion resided here, in another land, where her and her husband had escaped so many years prior."

Harlonngraith watched Kahlahnni and Samarra closely. He saw the Seer slowly squeeze her daughter's hand in reassurance. Samarra turned away from Harlonngraith and stared at her mother for several minutes before complete astonishment crossed her face. "You're the Seer." It was not a question.

"Yes." The answer was simple but held so much meaning.

"And you told him his Champion was here?"

"Yes."

Harlonngraith felt something within him shift as he watched her face fill with panic. Samarra stood knocking over her chair. "And I—and I," she stuttered. "I am his Champion?"

"Yes."

This time there was no one blocking her exit as she fled from the room.

Harlonngraith was expecting it and had stood, his own chair clattering to the floor.

"No," Evan interceded. "It is our turn. We allowed you to tell your story, your way. Now it is our turn."

Harlonngraith went to argue but backed down. "Very well."

"Get some rest. You have lost blood. There is a spare bedroom, last door on the left down the hall," offered Kahlahnni.

As they both left him to find his way down the hall and to the bedroom, all Harlonngraith could think about was the pain and fear his precious Samarra must be going through. He regretted all the pain he had caused and wished there was a different way.

Chapter 12

Samarra

It was bitterly cold as night had descended while Marra was being told the most fantastical story she had ever heard. Her mind tried to reconcile all she had been told but was shrinking away from it. How could it possibly be real? But why would her parents make this up? She shivered as she strode to the tree and pulled the knife that was still embedded in its trunk. The twin to this dagger was sitting on the kitchen bench. Marra studied the knife. Was it truly from another land? Another world? Her mind retreated from that thought, it was best to just think of it as another country for now.

The solar powered garden lights glowed dimly as she walked the short path and took a seat on the stone bench in the secluded garden. Marra crossed her arms and rubbed them with her hands, trying to stop her teeth from chattering. She refused to go back in the house and get a coat. The crunching of feet on stones alerted her to someone approaching, by the sound of it, it was two people approaching. "Go away," Marra said rudely, but didn't turn.

A heavy cloak was placed over her shoulders, and she raised her hand to pull it more securely around her when her hands encountered feathers. Marra held the cloak out with one arm and studied it in the dim light. It looked to be made of large, black, glossy feathers, yet the inside was soft on her exposed arms.

Her father and mother sat down on each side of her. Marra sat staring up at the statue in the garden. She noted the texture of the sculpture's clothing, more recalling it from memory than being able to see it in the low light. "Is that you?" she asked, turning slightly toward her mother.

"Yes," Lahnni's voice was gentle.

"And you both really come from a place called Segarris where Harley is the heir to the throne?"

"Yes," Evan answered this time.

"Why did you never tell me?"

"Because we hoped that this day would never come. That somehow your mother's visions would not come true. She sees what she sees, but people have free will and can change their path if they desire it."

Marra was shocked. "You have visions? I thought you were a tarot reader, skilled at reading body language?"

"I was trained to read body language. Tarot has always been just a way for me to hide my abilities. Though, my powers are limited here," Lahnni explained, as if it was all perfectly reasonable.

"Your powers?" Marra was bewildered.

"Your mother is what we call Gifted. Her brand had not been seen for generations."

"Stop." Marra stood and moved away from both of them. They watched her, concern on their faces. "This is a lot to take in."

"Yes," answered Lahnni.

Marra blew out her breath. "How about you just tell me your story? Where you grew up, how you met? Why you are here? And where do I fit into all of this?"

"I think that is a good idea, but wouldn't it be better if we didn't all freeze out here and went back inside? I have sent Harlonngraith to rest, so it will just be us."

"Harlonngraith," Marra said the name out loud. "Evannderth, Kahlahhni, what is it with all the long names and double letters? Though Mum's name sounds different from the others."

"Your mother's name comes from her people. There are regions in the country of Segarris, they used to be their own countries but were conquered and signed treaties to be provinces within Segarris. Each country had its own culture, heritage, and like Earth, has many different appearances. There are four groups of people that live within Segarris."

A sudden thought occurred to her. "How is it that Harley can speak the same language?"

"It is something we have discussed often over the years," Lahnni answered. "Our best guess is that one land developed first, and when the portal was discovered, they entered that land and either established a community there or gained power. The accent is different, but many of the words are English. Though the advancement on Earth has been faster. Think of Segarris as several centuries behind, no mechanical discoveries yet. Horses are the favored mode of transport for the wealthy and there is no running water."

"So, no equality? Stuck in the dark ages?"

"There is still racism, just like here, but sexism is not as rife. There have been powerful queens, the priestesses wield as much control as their counterparts, and your mother's people lead the way in having an equal number of men and women sitting on their council."

"And women can be the Champion and fight for their Challenger?"

"It has never been done, but yes, as far as I understand it, it is accepted," Evan answered.

"If you are a Seer and you saw that I was the Champion can you see if I win?" Marra turned to face her mother.

"I cannot see your fate. I have never been able to see your destiny. There has only ever been a foreboding and a need to make you..." Her voice trailed off.

"A need to make me what?" Marra demanded.

Evan stood and moved to her. He took her upper arms in each hand. "A need to have you as capable as I could make you." His voice was soft. "If I could have wished for you to have a different life, I would have. I would have wished for you to run free, and to make your own choices."

"You could have ignored mother's visions and hid me. Would Harley have found me if you hadn't have helped?" Marra's anger was rising. Everything she had known was a lie. Her entire life had been to be trained to be sent to another land and fight and possibly die. For what? For people she didn't know, or care who she was?

"Faffia, I am sorry," Evan said sadly. "We did what we thought was right."

"But you said before that we can change our fates, we are not bound by what mother sees." She knew her voice sounded desperate.

"Samarra," Lahnni used her full name. "When the Gods intervene we must obey. You have been called to be Champion and we were given the gift of being your parents."

"What happens if I choose not to fight? If I stay here instead?"

"Harlonngraith will be slain and Tommofey and Darria will have control of our homeland." Lahnni's words were blunt. "There will be darkness. Something that is hidden will be set free. What that is I do not know."

"And if I go and fight and die?" Marra asked, even though she could guess the answer.

"The same thing. The prince dies and darkness reigns."

"And if I go and win?"

"You live, he lives, and what is hidden is revealed, but after that is unclear. The balance between the two brothers is perfect at the moment. Choices must be made for both sides."

"You are not very comforting today," Marra complained.

This made her father smile sadly.

"If I go and fight, Harley and Segarris have a chance; if I don't, he dies." Marra summed up the conversation. She looked to her mother to find her brown eyes full of tears. Marra's heart lurched, and she realized that her anger and resentment were leaving and being replaced with compassion. "Oh, Mum, don't cry." Marra hurried to her mother and sat down on the bench beside her, covering her with the black feathered cloak and hugging her.

Lahnni whispered into the night. "We did all we could to keep you safe. We have given you every chance of survival, and instilled in you courage and kindness. But in the end, you must make this decision. No one will force you. Everything about the series of tasks is to do with character. To prove all that enter the Challenger's Arena four months from now will be worthy."

Marra recalled her dream of the night before. She had been surrounded by sets of weighing scales. All finally balanced, but with nothing on them. She dismissed the strange thought and sighed heavily. It was too much to take in. But she wanted to know it all. "Let's go inside and you can tell me your story."

Harlonngraith

"Aren't you supposed to be resting?" Marra asked as she walked back into the kitchen.

Harlonngraith turned from staring at the stove top. He was holding the kettle, that he had just filled with water, but couldn't figure out how to heat it. "I didn't know how long you were going to be out there, so I was going to put water on for tea."

Samarra looked at him for a moment. "Do you even know how to make tea?"

"Well, no, but I was willing to try to figure it out."

She shook her head and smiled. "I like that you are willing to learn, even if it is the simple things."

"If we think we don't need to continue to learn, even the small things, how can we grow and understand the world better?"

They were joined by Lahnni and Evan.

"I am making tea, if anyone would like one?" he asked.

"Yes, please," they both replied.

"Stupendous. Now if someone can only teach me how."

Samarra looked at him. "You can't walk around in a blanket the rest of the time you are here. You need a new top." She bit her lip as she picked up the blood-soaked shirt. "Dad might have something that fits," she said but didn't sound convinced.

"Hang on," Lahnni spoke as she hurried out of the room. "Here," she announced as she walked back in holding up Harlonngraith's dark blue sweater.

"Why do you have that? You have been doing his laundry?" Samarra was astounded.

"Well, of course, I have. Think about it. He is the prince of my homeland and..." Lahnni paused for affect Harlonngraith was positive. "He would have no clue how to turn a washing machine on."

This made Harlonngraith blush. "I did offer to learn," he defended himself as he handed the kettle over to Samarra and dragged the sweater over his head, being careful not to move his arm too much.

"You can teach him to make tea," announced Lahnni. "We will be in the lounge waiting for you both. It is time you learned everything."

Evan followed his wife into the lounge and left the two of them alone. Harlonngraith watched as Samarra plugged the kettle into the wall. "The cups are there." She pointed to the wooden thing that looked a little like a tree that had ceramic mugs hanging from it.

"Would you like a cup?" he asked as he carefully removed three mugs from the holder.

"Yes, please."

Harlonngraith placed a fourth mug where he had the others lined up.

"Can you get the milk out of the fridge?" she asked him, her voice a little less frosty than before.

He did what he was instructed. "Samarra, I need to say something," he started, then stopped. Not quite sure of what he wanted to say next. "I actually considered never telling you any of this and just staying here with you," he blurted out.

"You did?" she looked surprised.

"Yes, I could just become Harley and you Marra, and we could live in peace here. Never having to worry about scheming half-brother's, war, politics, keeping all the factions of my court happy, and sending you to what could be your death and ultimately mine."

She went to speak, but he held up his hand to forestall her. "But it is not who I am. I cannot do that to my people, to the many who rely on me. I have to trust that your mother's visions show that I am the better choice to rule. I will not force you to go with me. Hear your mother out and then make your decision. My duty compels me to return, but it need not do that to you."

"What happens if I don't go with you?" she asked.

He frowned and watched as she poured the now boiling water into the mugs. "I am not sure. I can find many in my ranks who will fight for me, who are almost your equal, but I do not know if they will be allowed as my Champion. There are many things that remain a mystery. I may forfeit my claim if I try to turn up with someone else, but I will take that risk to keep you safe if you so choose."

Rather than answer him, she changed the subject. "I am sorry about your arm."

He went to move to hold her, but she took a step back, causing him to stop. "My arm is fine, do not concern yourself." He tried to make light of it.

The tea was made and there was nothing left to do but follow Samarra into the lounge room and sit where he was told. Harlonngraith sipped the hot beverage and remained quiet. Evan had been right before when he had said that it was their turn to explain their story. Harlon-ngraith was just grateful that he would be privy to hear it from the Seer and the Captain.

Kahlahnni wasted no time as she cleared her throat, gaining everyone's attention. "I was raised in a small town in the north of Segarris where everyone looked like Evannderth and was suspicious of those who appeared different. My parentage is unknown." Her voice was soft, but underneath there was strength, as if the pain of the past could no longer reach her. "I was bullied by many and ignored by everyone else, except one woman who worked in the kitchens of the orphanage I grew up in. Cellecia was kind and always looked out for me. It wasn't until I was much older and had run away that I realized how much her and her husband had protected me over the years. She got me a job serving a Lady in a place where they weren't cruel; not welcoming, but not cruel. Cellecia's husband returned from the war and took her away and I thought I would never see them again, but the Lady I served died when I was fourteen and Emmitten, Cellecia's husband, came and threatened the person I was supposed to be passed to and took me away. I lived with their family for the next four years until the day of my branding."

The room remained quiet as Kahlahnni stopped and took a sip of her tea. "My visions have always been with me, but they grew stronger as I aged. I can learn many things by looking at someone, mostly it is basic feelings. But when I touch someone and they have strong emotions, I can receive powerful, clear visions. Sometimes I can direct the vision to what I want to see. The first terrifying prediction I saw was when the orphanage bully cornered me and broke my thumb. I saw him falling to his death surrounded by fire."

Harlonngraith noticed Kahlahnni's hands tighten around her mug, as if seeking the warmth from it for comfort.

"It was a sad and lonely existence, but I was so young and self-absorbed and didn't realize just how cared for and accepted I was by Cellecia and her family." She looked at her husband and smiled gently. "Evan came to town with the priest for the branding ceremony. It was the first time I had seen people who weren't all fair. None looked like me, but they did have darker tones. Evan held a meeting for all the supplicants and it was the first time in my life I felt seen."

Evan returned her smile and took her hand. "I remember it well. You were so beautiful. Young, sad, and innocent. You walked hunched over, as if hoping to shrink into the background, and you barely spoke above a whisper, if at all."

"My life changed the next day forever." Lahnni spoke simply.

"How?" asked Samarra, clearly caught up in the story as much as Harlonngraith was.

"The boy who broke my thumb and tormented me in the orphanage was a soldier and had arrived with Evan. The day of the branding ceremony dawned and all I could focus on was not being branded a Servant. I didn't want to be forever owned by someone."

"So, essentially, a slave?" Samarra asked, shocked. She looked at Harlonngraith. "You condone slavery?"

He held up his hands as if to ward off her ire. "I don't condone anything. The branding is done by the priests and is determined by the Gods. It is completely out of my control."

Evan interrupted all of them. "I was there as the leader of the soldiers but was also working with one of the order of the priesthood as there is something not right with the branding ceremony. People like the man who attacked Lahnni should never have been branded soldiers, but it was becoming more and more common, and I was hoping to find a pattern."

Samarra gasped. "You were attacked?"

Lahnni nodded. "But we have jumped ahead a little. Everyone took their turn at being branded and I was last. Unbeknown to me, everyone, bar a few, knew I would be branded a Roamer, the common name for the Pomaikka." She closed her eyes for a few moments and Harlonngraith wondered if she was reliving the occasion. "It did not go to plan and was quite traumatic. The brand didn't work the first time and the second time was excruciating. But I was eventually branded and everyone, including me, once it was explained, assumed it was the brand of the Roamer."

"It's not?" asked Samarra. "What is it then?"

"It is the brand of the Gifted, supposedly those touched by the Gods. So rare that generations pass without it being seen. But Evan knew what it was." She took another sip of tea. "I needed space. I was in pain, and I had no clue what being a Roamer meant, and if anything, I felt more isolated. I went to my safe space, a barn loft and hid, but the man that tormented me found me. He threatened me and his intent to cause me harm was clear. I tried to get away from him and started a fire by accident. I hurt my-self while trying to escape and brought the ladder down with me. He ordered me to help him, but I didn't." Lahnni's voice was emotionless, she stared straight ahead. "I had felt his touch and knew he was bad. He would hurt me and others. I didn't get the ladder; instead, I let him fall to his death as the burning barn collapsed. He had convinced me that no one would believe what had happened and I ran away."

Surprisingly she looked to Harlonngraith. "If I ever return to Segarris, I will face the consequences of taking a soldier's life."

Harlonngraith spoke from the heart. He could imagine a battered and bruised, scared young woman who had clearly been tormented all her life. "I pardon you for any crime you have committed in Segarris. I am sorry that you were not protected by our laws."

"Thank you." She looked to her daughter. "How you doing with all of this?"

Samarra's eyes shone with unshed tears and Harlonngraith's heart beat faster to see his beloved in pain. He wished he could ease it but knew she would not allow it at this time. "I wish you didn't have to live through any of it," Samarra answered fiercely.

Lahnni smiled reassuringly. "It made me who I am. There are still answers I seek but am not sure I will find. Anyway, let me shorten this story or we will be here all night. I struggled through the forest that ran adjacent to our town and followed the stream until I found a place I could rest. I fell twice and ended up with damage to my hands and knees and knocked myself out. By the time your father rescued me I was in a bad way. My brand was infected to complicate things further."

"She was a mess," Evan agreed, grinning at his wife. "And understandably completely wary of me and all I represented. She refused to return to the village, and I knew she needed to get to her people, as the brand of the Gifted was too important to ignore so I offered to help her find someone to aid her. After several events and being attacked, she finally admitted to knowing things she shouldn't."

Lahnni took up the story again. "He took me to the closest city, and we found the Pomaikka; eventually, we found the right ones who knew what to do with me and they took me in. I said goodbye to Evan, though it secretly broke my heart, for I had fallen madly in love with him, and was taken to the Settlement, the only city of the Roamers. Most live like the gypsies of old on Earth. They live in caravans or on river boats. But there is one central city where only those with Roamer blood can go."

Samarra interrupted the story. "Did you feel the same, Dad?" she asked.

"Your mother was young and innocent and my heart longed to protect her. She was brave and resilient even after all the pain. The suffering she endured as we approached the city, with all those people's emotions closing in on her was hard to watch. I would not admit it to myself for a long time, but yes, she had made a place in my heart that years later made me cast aside everything I had worked for." He looked at her lovingly.

Lahnni went on. "Years passed quickly, and while I had found my people, I had not found my place. I was trained and learned to control my Gift and emotions. But I was still an outsider, it was just now I was an important and sometimes feared outsider, but I still felt like a freak who didn't belong. I met your father again when I arrived at the capital of Segarris. They are twin cities, separated by a river. The palace, where Harlonngraith lives, is in one section, and across the river is the old palace, where the cast-off queen, Lady Darria, lives. Evan was working for the queen, by pretending to work for Lady Darria. They knew she was hiding things but did not know what. He asked me to do a reading for her and out of friendship to him I agreed. That is where I discovered she was pregnant and saw Harlonngraith and his brother Tommofey on the dais with shadowy figures beside them. One of those shadowy figures turned out to be you, Marra."

Before anyone could interrupt, Lahnni went on. "I would not tell Darria all I saw, but she could see I was valuable to her goals so sent Evan away and drugged me. He blew his cover to rescue me and took me to the palace. I met your mother, Harlonngraith, and quickly realized that while she hadn't locked me up like Darria, it was a possibility if I didn't perform the way she wished. I fell pregnant with Marra and knew that she would be used as a pawn to make me use my powers and that we were in danger. So, we escaped. Evan gave up his whole life's work to protect me and his child, and chose to live in a land that is totally alien in every way. But we carved a life and kept Marra safe. It was only once she was born that I knew it wasn't over. My powers are weakened here, but I get glimpses every now and then. I knew the day Tommofey declared he would challenge. The day we had worked toward but dreaded had arrived."

Lahnni took a breath and turned to Samarra. "What I haven't said is what came to me when Tom issued the challenge. You need to be trained. There is one more thing you must learn, and neither your father nor I can teach it. Even though it pains me more than you will ever understand, I urge you to go to Segarris with Harlonngraith." Kahlahnni turned to the prince. "You must take her to the Pomaikkan's."

The room fell quiet. Harlonngraith recognized that they were each lost in their own thoughts.

"I will go," Samarra spoke softly into the silence. "I will go and meet the Pomaikka as you ask. If you think they can train me further, then I shall go." Samarra took in a deep breath and Harlonngraith held his. "But I will not commit to fighting and possibly dying for something I have not seen or lived. For a nation that keeps slaves, no matter how they are labelled, is not something I want to fight for." She expelled it sharply. "That is all I can offer at this time."

As Lahnni and Evan stood to hug Samarra, Harlonngraith should have been elated. She had not said no. Yet, instead, all he felt was dread. He was about to drag the woman he had come to love into an environment she had not been raised in. Though she was astounding in so many ways, would she survive the politics of his homeland?

Chapter 13

Samarra

Her sleep had again been troubled. Since coming through the portal two days prior, it had become worse. Nightmares plagued her, but she never remembered them. Harley told her that she murmured and cried out in her sleep, which was keeping him awake. Both now had dark circles under their eyes. Thankfully, no one saw them. Since the moment they had arrived in this strange land, they had been isolated as plans were put in place and their identity kept hidden.

They were staying on the second floor of an old and what looked to be abandoned chapel on the palace grounds while things were being put in motion. From the quick glimpse Marra had seen as they were hurried through on their arrival, the lower floor was filled with dust and cobwebs, but the second floor, which consisted of one large room, had been cleaned until it sparkled.

It turned out that her mother's gift was capable of opening the portal between worlds without help of any kind. Something they had all sworn to keep secret. No one would ever know, except the four of them. Absolutely no one.

As arranged, Evan had snuck in and left a note for Zussya to find when he did his weekly checks, which had been pre-arranged when Harley had stepped through the portal to find her. The note had told him that two would be coming through and that they would need to visit the Roamers. They were to be disguised as travelers who were seeking a cure for an unknown disease but were keeping their distance from others as it may be contagious.

They had been set up in the chapel and their only contact had been Zussya, who had been thrilled to meet Marra. He had explained there were a few more things to take care of but had spread a rumor that the chapel was being used by a couple who were seeking penance before they journeyed to the Roamer in search of a cure. As they were rich, and the church was always looking for generous donations, he had agreed to find them somewhere away from prying eyes. The Queen had agreed, not really interested in the hovel of a chapel that was hidden from the rest of the surrounding well-tended gardens, she was busy playing her games of politics and trying not to fret about having no word from her son regarding his search for his Champion.

Marra traced the scar on Harley's arm. "Does it hurt?" she asked softly, still embarrassed by her behavior that day.

"Don't worry about it," Harley replied as he covered her hand with his own. "I deserved it."

"No, you didn't. Dad and I spent so much time working on my temper. I thought I had it under control."

He lifted her hand and kissed it. "I pushed you with my impatience and handled that whole situation badly. I was a complete idiot. It makes me wince now as I think back to my stupid answers. I completely provoked you. It was not kind, nor gentle, when I told you who I was. It was arrogant and wrong and I hope that you will forgive me for the pain I caused."

She twisted her hand in his and brought his palm to her lips. "I will forgive you if you forgive me?" she whispered.

"Easily. You were forgiven the moment you did it. Just don't go throwing knives at me when the guards are around, they might not understand."

This made her giggle.

"Hey, you know what?" he asked.

"What?"

"I haven't collected on you losing the game that day."

"What are you talking about?"

"The deal was that if you hit the target in the center I had to answer your questions honestly. Which I did." He inclined his head at her. "But if you missed you had to give me whatever prize I wanted."

"Well, yes."

"You." He reached out and drew her to him with a single finger under her chin. "Missed."

His breath was hot on her face, and she felt herself grow flustered. Marra bit her lower lip as she considered her response. "But did I miss?" she drew out her answer.

"You missed the target."

"Ah, yes, but I never said what my target was. What happens if I changed my target through the game?"

He let go of her chin and took her face in both his powerful hands. His lips brushed hers as he spoke. "Did you change your target during the game, my queen?"

"No," she breathed the word out.

"Then I would like to claim my prize."

"Now?"

"Now."

Harley kissed her, his lips brushing hers gently, his tongue finding hers. It was tender and beautiful. He pulled back from the kiss and watched her. "You are perfect."

Marra reached up and placed her hands on his chest. "Prince Harlonngraith, you may be the most perfect man in two worlds."

"Pretty words will get you everywhere, but not out of me claiming my prize."

She frowned. "Was the kiss not your prize?"

He laughed. "Hardly." He dropped his hands from her face and moved them down to the belt that held her robe in place. He untied the sash and pushed the robe from her shoulders to expose her naked body. Harley took a step back and studied her.

Marra caught herself smiling wryly as she placed her hands on her hips.

"You are my prize," he claimed. "Every inch of you belongs to me."

"Really? And what do you plan on doing with your prize," she asked as if challenging him.

"Devouring it. Every single, delectable inch of it, bite by bite." Harley licked his lips. "Now, climb up onto that bed," he ordered in that low rumbling voice that always made her melt.

"Yes, your majesty." She curtsied primly and walked past him.

He smacked her arse hard enough to make her yelp but not to hurt. "A smart mouth will not be tolerated in my court." He fake scowled at her.

Changing tact, Marra turned back to the prince and dropped to her knees. "What about a clever mouth?" She reached out and pulled the strings of his trousers, gaining her access to what was clearly an already semi-aroused cock. She pulled his pants down far enough to gain full access and grabbed the base of his cock firmly while she ran her tongue around the rim making him hiss softly. Slowly, Marra took him into her mouth. Alternating sucking and stroking as she did. Within seconds he was rock hard.

Marra continued to stroke firmly as she released him from her mouth and kissed her way down his thigh and up again until she reached his balls. She took one gently into her mouth and rolled it around, slowly increasing the pressure, when she felt him tense, she let go and moved to the other, slowly sucking him in and enjoying the sensations she knew she was causing. She squeezed his cock harder and increased the pressure as she again drew him into her mouth, swirling her tongue around the tip.

Harley moaned and pushed his hips forward. He buried his hands in her hair but did not try to hold her in place. He was allowing her to set the pace. The way this man would give up control as easily as he took it was such a huge turn on.

Marra alternated between sucking, stroking, and running her finger over the tip of his beautiful cock, with ever growing speed and pressure. "Samarra, you need to stop," he said quickly.

But this only urged her on. She sucked harder and faster, completely holding him in place with her hands.

"Samarra," Harley warned, but it was too late. The first spurts of warm liquid hit her throat and she swallowed. He groaned loudly and twisted her hair further. She slowed her action but didn't stop as his cock pulsated in her mouth and she swallowed all he gave her. With a shudder, he slowly pushed her away. She looked up to find his eyes glazed. Marra grinned.

Harley held out his hand and helped her back to her feet. She kissed him once before she walked past, slapped him on the arse, and headed to the large canopied bed. "Now, what were you saying about claiming your prize?"

Harley laughed and began to tug his trousers off. "You, my queen, are so brazen." He managed to do it in far quicker time than she thought possible. Harley began to walk toward her. "It is one of the many reasons I love you."

The room stilled as they both stopped. Slowly Marra turned to look fully at the man of her dreams. They were both exposed physically, and emotionally. "You love me?" she asked.

He rushed to her and gathered her in his arms, kissing the top of her head. "Yes, I love you. How could I not love you? You are sweet, kind, smart, funny, sassy, talented, and tall, and the fact you can kick my ass and do it without hesitation is a bit of a turn on." He winked.

Marra let the words sink in. He loved her, for her. For being strong, and capable, and not delicate, and needing to be rescued.

"I love you in spite of you being a prince."

"Ooof, so the title doesn't rock your world?"

"The title frightens me. I love you without the title. I love you for learning how to make tea, for being there when I can't sleep, for wanting to be more when you already have everything. I love you, Harlonngraith for you. Now come and claim your prize."

Chapter 14

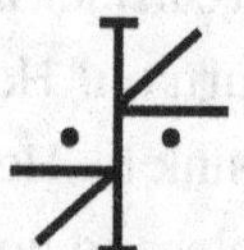

Harlonngraith

"Why are you insisting on all this secrecy?" Harlonngraith could hear his mother complain. He smiled to himself. He was quite enjoying this little moment before surprising her that he had returned. A select troop of his personal bodyguard had been assembled and sent out in two groups. One would travel in front of them and one behind. Both keeping a distance, but there if circumstances changed or speed rather the secrecy was required. None of them knew anything other than they were escorting important people to the Pomaikka on the request of their prince.

Harlonngraith watched Samarra hitch up her skirt for what must be the tenth time in the past half turning. The large, cumbersome dresses of his people were a far cry from what he had come to learn were yoga pants that she favored at home. The only thing her father had agreed to allow her to take were good lace up boots. Her mother had given her a different gift all together, and it was currently tightly packed and in one of the saddle bags of their pack horse.

He made his way down the stairs just before the door of the chapel was pushed open. The cross face of Queen Anzhellika quickly changed to shock and then joy when she saw her eldest son for the first time since he had left to find his Champion. As far as she knew he was somewhere up in the mountains near Wasshun. "What? How?" she exclaimed as she hurried toward him.

Arch Deacon Zussya quickly shut the chapel doors so no one could witness the reunion.

"Hello, Mother," Harlonngraith said warmly, but he was uncomfortable to find his thoughts regarding his mother had shifted since being with Kahlahnni and Evannderth. He had always admired his mother and all she had overcome, but now everything was tainted with a seed of doubt. She was, after all, human and flawed, but he had never considered how. She loved, protected, and guided him, but now he wondered whether it was love or manipulation.

"My darling boy, how are you here?" She embraced him tightly.

Harlonngraith returned her hug. "It is good to see you," he said honestly. "I have been searching for my Champion, who I have not yet found." He told half the truth. "But I have been in contact with the Seer Kahlahnni and she has told me to search amongst the Pomaikka, so that is where I go. But I could not leave today without visiting."

Anzhellika stepped back abruptly, "You saw the traitor? I have had people searching for them for over twenty years."

Those words made Harlonngraith's heart constrict. "Why?"

"Why? Because she has the ability to see what is coming, to forewarn of disaster. It is her duty to serve the crown." The queen's voice was matter of fact. "And the Captain is invaluable. His knowledge in training troops has been sorely missed, his insights into people were always on point. and he threw it all away for love." She almost spat out those final words.

Harlonngraith kept his face neutral and hoped Samarra, who was listening from the bedroom upstairs, was going to keep her temper and not storm down and insist on the queen taking back her rude words. He considered the words and concluded that from his mother's point of view they were true. She was thinking of ways to protect her nation and children. "Captain Evannderth did desert his role, I will agree, but Seer Kahlahnni is not a Servant. Her role as Gifted was given by the Gods, not the crown, and she can choose to do whatever she wants with that power. I believe what she has chosen is to serve all of Segarris, not just the powerful."

"Really?" Anzhellika's response dripped with sarcasm. "She has served the people of Segarris by going into hiding for two decades?"

With effort, Harlonngraith bit back his harsh response. "She has done what she feels was required by the Gods." He stopped short from asking his mother if she knew what the Gods wanted, because he sure as hell didn't. "I am here to find out if you need anything. Has there been word if Tommofey has found his Champion?"

"He is not keeping his movements secret. He headed east, toward Mammylah and he offers gold to find the best fighter in the land." Her voice was filled with disdain.

"Well, I guess that's one way to do it," Harlonngraith said with little inflection.

"We have someone keeping tabs on him."

"Good. Is there anything else I need to be aware of?"

"It has been a full year since the last raid on the Island of Lobbregath, the council, under the guidance of General Ittaie, have brought half the troops who were bivouacked there, back to the main outpost in Pluddgish to have them re-outfitted, rested and reassessed for duties. Once that is done, they will be re-assigned and the other half of the troops will be brought back. As normal a small troop will be left to signal and defend if the filthy Trioswan return."

"Which we know they will until we defeat them completely." Harlonngraith spoke with annoyance. It was one thing he hoped to accomplish in his lifetime. The end of the ongoing fight to keep control of the Islands of Lobbregath.

"I am sorry to interrupt this family reunion, but you mustn't stay much longer, your majesty," Arch Deacon Zussya pointed out.

Anzhellika gave her son a tight hug. "Be safe and find that damned Champion. I didn't sacrifice everything to get you here to lose it all now. And when you get back, we will have a serious discussion about where you found the Seer and captain and what we are going to do about it."

"Yes, mother," he said tightly. Everything she had just said set off alarm bells in his head. Had she always been this ambitious and forceful? Was he noticing it now or was she just this way because of the upcoming trial and she was concerned for him? Did she care about him dying or her plans being ruined? "I will try to get word to you when I can. If not, I will meet you at the Challenger's Arena on the appointed day."

She kissed his cheek and swept from the room. No I love you's were exchanged. It was painfully different to the goodbyes he had witnessed just a few days earlier when Samarra had left her parents.

Zussya let the queen out, but did not follow her. Instead, he closed the door and approached the prince. "Everything is set. You leave as the sun goes down, when the streets will be busy. The river boat is ready. They do not know who you are. They will feed you and get you to the Settlement, but have been told to leave you alone. Do not go outside your cabin, for anything."

"Thank you, my friend." Harlonngraith clasped the Arch Deacon's forearm. "You serve the people of Segarris well."

Arch Deacon Zussya bowed. "Thank you, Your Highness."

"One thing before you go. Evan spoke about you and he's looking into disturbing patterns with the branding ceremony. I am wondering whatever came of that?"

Zussya grimaced. "I ran into a dead end about eight years ago, around the same time your brother was sent to me, and I became distracted."

"Fair enough, but I think if Evannderth thinks it important then we should perhaps begin to look into it again? Yes?"

"I will gather my notes and quietly start making new inquiries."

"Excellent. Perhaps there will be new data now more time has passed."

"I will do my best."

"That's all I ever require."

"Your Highness, may I say that I wish you all the best. I trust that what you are doing is required, but I must admit to not understanding why it is imperative you take the young lady to the Pomaikka now?"

"I told you, this is important. You need to believe I am doing everything asked of me to prove my worthiness to the Gods to guide my Champion to me. If Kahlahnni says this is what I must do, I will not falter in my task."

"Wish the lady well and may your journey be incident free. I will have someone stay outside the Settlement in case you need to get me a message quickly."

"Thank you. I think you have thought of everything. You would have made an excellent general, marshalling my soldiers."

"I just marshal the Gods soldiers instead."

The Arch Deacon left and Harlonngraith was alone with his thoughts. There was much going on, but nothing he could control, and it frustrated him. Everything now relied on the beautiful woman listening from the second floor. And though he was keeping his promise of not talking about her being his Champion he thought about it often. He was going to have to learn patience fast if he didn't want to cause trouble between them.

"Well?" asked Harlonngraith as he climbed the stairs to find Samarra sitting there, her hands clasped tightly together in her lap.

"Well, what?" she replied.

"Well, that was my mother." Now he said it he wasn't sure he wanted to have this conversation. She had said several insulting things about Samarra's parents.

"She's quite ambitious," Samarra observed.

This made him grunt. "More than I had ever noticed."

Chapter 15

Samarra

The first few days of being locked in a room with the man you loved were just as wonderful as Marra had thought they would be. They had talked about anything and everything. They had discovered each other's ticklish spots and told each other their childhood dreams. But now it felt like the cabin walls were pushing inwards. The river boat was owned by a Roamer family and they had given up their master bedroom for the gold the Arch Deacon had offered. But Roamers were small people, the shortest race in Segarris, and the cabin was not built for the tall and broad prince and the only slightly smaller Marra.

They were beginning to get in each other's way and it was made worse by the fact that Mara was continuing to disturb their sleep with her ever increasing nightmares. Images of her entering the large stone arena mixed with watching Harley die with one of her own daggers in his heart, while she stood over him with bloody hands. The images were frightening, and she continually fretted. She missed her mother's comfort. Lahnni had been the only one able to soothe Marra's nightmares.

Marra lay still, facing the wall, her back to Harley, who was sitting on the only seat that ran underneath the tiny window. *Don't cry,* she told herself, as her sadness spiraled. *You are far from home and have no sleep. You are being taken to who knows where and at the end of it all you will be expected to make a life altering decision. You must choose to fight for the man you love and perhaps die, which will also result in his death, or you could fight and win, which means you have taken another's life, or you could refuse to fight and someone not as skilled as you will represent Harley and he will more than likely die anyway. All of those choices totally suck,* she complained in her head.

Her emotions were overwhelming, and she closed her eyes against it all, but quickly snapped them open as her mind became filled with images of symbols, and daggers, and the sound of whispering. Was she going crazy? Could she hold on for three more days until they arrived at the Settlement?

A tear slid over her cheek and Marra sniffed softly, hoping not to disturb Harley. She heard him move and the mattress dipped as he settled next to her. "Talk to me," Harley urged. "I want to be here for you."

"I am fine," she lied.

"No, you aren't."

"It's nothing." She tried to dismiss it.

"Samarra, stop with this." His voice held an edge. "I love you and want to help, but you have to talk to me."

Something irritated her about the tone of his voice and she flipped over and sat up. "You can't make me talk to you, you know?"

This made him sit up. "What?"

"Just because you want me to do something doesn't mean I have to do it," she said with a touch more aggression than she had intended.

Marra watched Harley open and close his mouth twice and realized he was doing all he could to keep his own temper in check. "You know I love that you are strong, independent, and can totally kick my butt and that I have no intention of ever making you do anything you don't want, so why are you saying that?" His voice was calm.

Without warning, she burst into tears and Harley looked completely baffled and slightly alarmed. "I didn't mean to make you cry."

"You didn't," she wailed.

"Shhh, come here." He held out his arms and she scooted over until she was cuddled against him, her long legs bent over the top of his. Harley stroked her hair and held her while she cried.

"I am exhausted. I can't even close my eyes without seeing horrible images of you," she told him between sobs.

Harley began to hum softly, while he continued to stroke her hair. Marra felt herself begin to relax, her tears subsiding, and then he began to sing, his voice quiet and more musical than she thought possible. He had a beautiful voice, but what was more astounding was he was singing the same lullaby her mother used to sing to her, and before Marra could think further, her eyelids grew heavy, and when she closed her eyes all she saw was darkness, no horrid images there to bother her. And she gratefully fell asleep.

Chapter 16

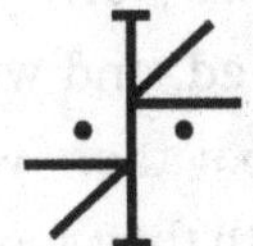

Harlonngraith

The days had all begun to blur into one, but by Harlonngraith's calculations they were mere turnings away from their destination. He looked over at the sleeping woman and smiled. She was finally having restful sleep now that he sang to her and when she became restless in the night he would hum and that seemed to calm her. Harlonngraith's throat was sore, but it was well worth it to see the dark circles on her gorgeous face slowly disappear.

Harlonngraith was grateful but tired. Marra had now managed to have several nights of full sleep, but he had not, as he was continually waking when she moved or whimpered as his heart reached out to her. So, he sang or hummed, depending on the time of day or night. He tried to do it quietly so as not to disturb the other people on the boat.

It was dawn and the small window had its curtains drawn and had for the past day as they passed through more crowded villages and didn't want to chance someone catching a glimpse of his face by accident.

His silent musings were disturbed by the sound of voices muttering outside their door. Harlonngraith wondered what was going on. The owners of the boat had been respectful the entire journey; knocking once when there was food delivered, and when Harlonngraith or Samarra opened the door there was no one ever there, just the covered tray with their food, or a bowl and cloths for bathing.

But now there was nattering, and it was growing louder. It was only then that he realized that the boat was no longer moving. Harlonngraith wondered what had happened. Should he open the door? Perhaps he should speak to somebody through the door? They were so close to the Settlement.

The talking on the other side of the door grew louder, more urgent and he could make out a few words. They were speaking Pomaikkan and he wasn't sure whether their hosts knew that he could understand it. His guess was probably not. All he could make out was "soldiers" and "the bridge being blocked."

Harlonngraith tried to recall the geography of the area that he had studied while younger and figured that they were near the bridge leading into the town of Aviggay-illis which meant they were only half a turning from the Settlement. If his memory was correct, the bridge was a solid construction of stone and was wide enough to have carts cross going in both directions. The banks of the river were high, allowing a long, flat boat that the Roamer's used on the river system to pass under easily, even when there was heavy rain, which was rare out in this area.

In the end, he tapped on the door and asked, "Is everything fine?" in Pomaikkan.

There was silence on the other side for a moment, and then a hesitant voice answered, "Sir, there seems to be an issue with the bridge. Soldiers have hung large heavy chains from the bridge and no boats can pass and we don't know what to do. There are several boats ahead of us that have had to stop also. There is much yelling."

"I am coming out. Can someone go outside and see if they can discover anything else?"

Harlonngraith turned to find Samarra climbing out of bed. "I will go out and see what is happening. No one knows my face," she declared.

"True," he answered slowly.

He watched as Samarra took down the Roamer clothing she had hung up several days ago to allow the creases to drop. This would be the first time she wore it, as she had been wearing typical Segarrin clothing consisting of a simple full skirt with buttoned blouse. Samarra had refused to even try on anything he would classify as appropriate court attire as she didn't deem it necessary. He pulled out his long, heavy cloak from his pack and put it on, making sure the hood covered as much of his face as possible, but that he was still able to see.

He surreptitiously watched Samarra wiggle into the black, high-waisted full skirt, and tuck in the mulberry colored tunic in a beautiful shiny material. She made certain the sleeve cuffs were tied tightly so nothing would expose her wrist tattoos. She then put on a black vest with gold cord and laced it up at the front. In short time she had also put on hose and her ankle boots that she had brought from home. "Wow," he said and whistled. "You look amazing."

Samarra looked worried. "Do I look like I belong?"

He cocked his head and studied her, putting his longing to one side. "Yes, your coloring is lighter, but not that unusual that it will be commented on. Though your height will definitely tell everyone that someone had a dalliance with an *Eastern Segarrin sometime in your history."

"Good." She tucked her blue daggers into the pockets of her skirt. "Let's find out what the hold up is."

"They are saying that there are soldiers, and chains are blocking the bridge," he explained.

Samarra frowned. "Chains blocking the bridge? How?"

"I am only guessing, but they have hung them over the side. It's a narrow section of the river, probably why the bridge was built there. If it has been raining heavily of late, which I admit I didn't think to ask till now, the boats will have less clearance under the bridge and dangling thick, heavy chains could cause damage."

Harlonngraith opened the door to find the small corridor empty. He wondered if the family was on deck or had chosen to hide in their cabin. Making sure not to hit his head, he ducked and made his way to the outer door, his broad shoulders skimming the sides of the narrow hallway. Harlonngraith held the door open for Samarra to go through and kept it open so he could hear all that transpired.

"You guessed right." Samarra spoke quietly as she stood near the door. "It's exactly how you described it. We are in a wider section, but to the left side, with enough room for boats to pass on the right. Nothing is moving, but there are several soldiers on the bridge and a few more walking up and down the riverbank. One is coming now."

"Is the owner of our boat out there with you?" Harlonngraith asked as quietly as he could. He knew his deep voice carried further than most.

"Hang on."

Harlonngraith waited, trying to keep his patience in check. He didn't like not knowing what was going on. He could hear footsteps and the water lapping against the hull, voices in the distance, and a few birds squawking overhead.

Finally, Samarra spoke. "Our host is at the back of the boat, holding the rudder. It is a rudder, right?" she whispered.

Harlonngraith smiled to himself. It was good to see she didn't know everything. Sometimes he was overwhelmed with her sheer competence in everything. Here was something she knew nothing about, and it made him love her more, if that were possible.

"Excuse me, Sir," her voice spoke in a respectful tone. "What has happened to the bridge?"

"Nothing has happened to the bridge, you stupid Roamer wench. We are carrying out inspections and the chains make it easier to stop the boat and keep everyone behaving," he almost spat the words at her.

"Oh, I see. May I inquire how long will it take?"

"That depends on you. It takes many turnings to inspect a boat and things unfortunately get broken in the process, or you could gift us something and we might be able to forget that your boat was even here and lift the chains quickly."

"What happens if we have nothing to gift?" Samarra asked meekly.

"You are comely enough, even for a Roamer, I am certain you have something I am interested in."

Harlonngraith felt his temper rise. These men weren't soldiers. What they were doing was extortion and it was against the law. They had no right to be inspecting boats here, that was done in the harbors. His thoughts were interrupted by a woman's loud begging and crying, followed by a large splash.

"They just threw something overboard two boats up," Samarra whispered.

"Are they soldiers?" he asked.

"They are in uniform."

Harlonngraith realized that she wouldn't be able to answer that question as she wouldn't know a real uniform from a counterfeit one. He needed to know what was happening. "I am coming out. Move to the side," he said softly.

"Is that wise?" she asked, but it was too late. Samarra glared at him as she stepped to her left.

"Good morning, soldier." Harlonngraith spoke with a friendly tone while he took in all he could. What was the most shocking was this man truly was a soldier in his army. "Who authorized this little venture?"

The young man, no older than twenty, probably just out of training laughed. "That's none of your business. Pay up or step aside and prepare for inspection."

"Who is in charge here?"

"I don't have to tell you that."

"Actually, you do. By law you must identify your immediate superior when asked. And I am asking."

The soldier looked a little stunned. "Sergeant Correntin and Brother Lavee are in charge."

"You are a Branding force?"

"Yes." The soldier looked uncomfortable for a moment.

Harlonngraith had had enough of the back and forth. This boy was not going to be helpful in any way. "Go and get the priest or the sergeant. I want those chains raised and a full report into what is going on here."

The young man lifted his head and puffed out his chest. "And why would I do that for you?"

"Don't," Samarra warned softly.

But Harlonngraith had had enough, he lifted his hands and pulled back his hood. "Because I asked you to."

The rude young soldier smirked and crossed his arms over his now puffed chest. "And you are?"

Harlonngraith had always wanted to do this. It was rare that someone didn't know who he was. It was silly and a little immature, but the woman wailing and the soldiers laughing and threatening to throw more of her items overboard was making him angry. "I am Prince Harlonngraith." He paused for effect. "And I have a meeting with the Pomaikka that you are keeping me from."

The young man's bravado slid a few degrees and he hurriedly explained, "They are breaking their fast. The priest was not feeling well so we were told to be useful till midday meal."

Harlonngraith looked disdainfully around. "And this is a productive use of your time?"

The young man had the grace to blush.

"And tell me, would you have taken advantage of this woman if she had agreed to your terms?"

He became flustered. "I, uh—"

"If I discover any of these men have taken money or traded favors in any way with these citizens of my nation I will have them court marshalled."

"Sir?"

"Stop standing there gaping. My suggestion would be to spread the word and get those buffoons to stop harassing that poor woman. And get me someone in charge now."

The soldier stood his ground for a few more moments. "How do I know you are the prince?"

"How do you know I am not? Fetch someone and we shall see, but I would be quick about it."

With one final look of indecision, the soldier bowed and hurried toward the boat that all the yelling was coming from. Harlonngraith watched him gesture quickly down to their boat and then to the town. A small group of people had begun to gather at the bridge, the soldiers' antics were beginning to draw a crowd.

"I don't know if you should have done that." Samarra looked up at him. She looked beautiful in the early morning light, the rays of brittle sun showing the gold highlights in her medium brown hair. "Your impatience is going to get you in serious trouble one day."

"Pfft. How much trouble can I get in with you here to protect me?" He winked at her. "I am just glad that woman's wailing has ended."

"What will you do with this lot?"

"Their wages will be garnished to pay for anything that has been broken or destroyed. Obviously, if they took goods or money, they will be returned. If they have taken advantage of anyone physically, they will be court marshalled. A complete investigation into how this happened and who the ring leaders were will have to be done first. Until that time, this troop will be held here. Once we get to the Settlement, I will write my own report and send for a new Branding force from the closest city." Harlonngraith looked at the bridge and watched as the chains were being raised. No one had come to check on his claim that he was the prince, clearly just the threat of him being here was enough to stop this appalling behavior.

In a shorter time than Harlonngraith expected, both the priest and the sergeant came riding up to his boat, led by the soldier, now also sitting on a horse. All three dismounted and stood on the river bank and bowed. "Your Highness, please forgive my tardiness. I was not aware you were stopping by today," the sergeant spoke hastily.

"Clearly." Harlonngraith was in no mood for platitudes. "These soldiers are undisciplined and out of their jurisdiction. I want a full report to me at the Settlement by sundown. I will have orders for you at that time. Until then, round up these miscreants and have the town's guard keep an eye on them. There are to be no deserters."

The sergeant saluted him. "Yes, Your Highness."

"Do not disappoint me, Correntin, this is your command and I want answers." Something else occurred to Harlonngraith and he decided to act on it. "When you bring your report, I also want the Branding ledger."

"Your highness, that is highly unusual." The priest looked concerned.

Harlonngraith said nothing but stared at him until the priest looked away.

"I will bring it," agreed the sergeant.

"Stay a moment, Correntin." Harlonngraith looked to the priest and soldier. "Get the boats moving. By the time I finish speaking to the sergeant, I want to be on my way," he ordered.

Both men bowed, mounted, and rode away urging their horses into a canter. Harlonngraith turned back to the sergeant. "I also want this town's Branding ledger, but the priest does not need to know."

"Yes, Sir." The sergeant nodded.

"Good, now no boat moves but mine until full reports have been taken from everyone about what has occurred this morning. And whatever they threw overboard has been replaced. Do not fail me again, sergeant." Harlonngraith turned from the soldier and walked to the back of the boat where the owner stood trying to look anywhere but the prince. "You may pull out and leave. The rest of these boats will need to stay and answer questions.

Would you be so kind as to show both Lady Samarra and myself how your vessel works?"

Chapter 17

Samarra

Too many emotions warred within her, so rather than overreact she didn't react at all. Marra packed her belongings silently, she wrinkled her nose at the smell of some of them. They had been locked in this cabin for too long and she desperately needed a proper soak, just as much as her hair and clothing did.

"You have nothing to worry about," Harley assured her as she buttoned up the backpack. "You are the daughter of the Seer and Evannderth."

"That's what I do worry about. So much expectation. My parents seem to be legends and I have done nothing." She tried not to let her voice sound whiny.

Silence filled the cabin and Marra realized Harley was doing his best not to point out that she had been chosen for something significant, she had simply refused to accept it—the role of being his Champion. "To be honest, at this point, I will just accept them not throwing me out and allowing me to sit in warm water."

She looked over to the prince sitting on her bed. He grinned at her and winked. "Be careful what you wish for."

"What's that supposed to mean?" she asked, suddenly suspicious.

"Now, if I tell you, it will ruin all the fun."

"Oh, come on, there is so much here to adjust to. Give me a hint at least."

"Nope."

There was a polite tap on the cabin door. "Your Highness, we have arrived."

"Thank you," Harley responded cheerfully. "Remember who you are and where you come from. No one here can even operate one of those mobile phone things you are all so fond of."

This made her laugh. "How did you manage with everything?"

"I put many things in the need-to-know basket and I really didn't need to know many things."

"Wish I could do the same," she moaned.

"I wish many things but now I am not so sure that I would change anything."

This stopped Marra and her complaining. "Like what?"

"Well, I used to wish that Darria wasn't so power-hungry and had not raised Tommofey to try to claim the throne. They have titles and money, and it should have been enough. I also used to wish that my father had been able to love my mother and respect his country enough to not sleep with the ex-queen to have her fall pregnant." His beautiful gray eyes looked at her in frustration. "But once you start wishing or regretting, where do you stop? It changes nothing and doesn't show you what you should be appreciating. For without all of those moments that

I had no control over I wouldn't be here with you, the woman I love. And because of that, I would change nothing. So I accept what I must to have the things that I love."

Marra looked at the handsome man who looked at her with nothing but love and acceptance. He was her everything and she didn't know how she would live life without him if she chose not to fight for him and her replacement got them both killed, but there was something that still held her back. She wondered with all his responsibilities if the situations were reversed would he willingly put his life on the line for her?

A polite cough from the other side of the door interrupted any further conversation. "Would you like me to carry your bags, Your highness?"

"Thank you, but no. I will take the Lady's and my own packs." Marra went to speak but Harley stood and moved to take the bag from her. "Don't say anything. I rarely get to treat you the way you should be treated. Allow me to carry the packs of the Seer's daughter and love of my life."

Marra didn't argue she reached up and touched his face, running her thumb across his high cheekbone. "Thank you."

Samarra

The Settlement was not what she expected. Marra had been envisaging a landscape filled with colorful caravans like the gypsy's of old on Earth; instead, what she saw were many single story squat, square buildings with crenulated rooftops. They were built from something like the color of sandstone, for some reason reminding her of the stones that created the pyramids. As they disembarked from the long boat, many people turned to stare. Harley and her own height clearly gave them away as strangers. She tightened her grip on her cloak, not to ward off the cool breeze but the wary glances. Is this what it felt like to not fit in somewhere? She had at times felt out of place because of her height, but never anything like this. How had her mother survived years of this? She felt her shyness settle over her like the beautiful cloak she wore and hoped when the moment came, she wouldn't be too tongue tied to speak.

The dock area was a busy hub of people coming and going, many boats moored alongside the wide river on both sides. At the edge of the city that ran alongside the river was a dirt road that was filled with a multitude of different people. Once she was amongst that crowd, the feeling of people staring definitely eased. Between the road and the city stood a large wooden, square, raised platform. One lone man stood on the platform. "What's he doing?" Marra whispered as they walked in the direction of the platform.

"Waiting for one of the elders to come and decide his fate."

"His fate?" Marra halted. "What do you mean by that?"

"It is a little dramatic." Harley spoke quietly as he took her hand and tugged it to get her moving again. "But nothing to worry about. To enter the city without being one of the Pomaikka you must stand on the platform and wait for someone to come. You plead your case and they allow you to enter or not."

"And we have to do this?" she was not liking the idea of standing on the platform all that appealing.

"Technically, I don't. I am their prince and can go anywhere I choose, and if I were in a hurry I wouldn't bother, but showing everyone I am willing to play by the rules never hurt."

"Is everything political to you?" Her voice was a little sharper than she would have wanted.

He halted them in the middle of the traffic, which earned them several disgruntled comments. His eyes were serious. "You aren't political. I broke the rules for you."

"Because I am your Champion?" she asked.

"No, because I fell in love with you."

This gave her pause. Marra was so caught up in her life and decisions she never truly considered Harley's life and though it looked like a glamorous life on the surface it was filled with difficulties and never knowing who to trust. Everyone wanted something from the prince.

"Come. It isn't safe standing out in the open like this."

"Why?"

"You stand on the edge of the Settlement in your mother's feather cape, with a man who looks remarkably like the prince. There are always people willing to sell information, they don't care to who."

"What do we do?" asked Marra.

"Stand on the platform and wait. With that cloak on I can't see us waiting for long. At this moment in time, I doubt anyone will even register my existence."

Marra followed Harley to the platform and climbed the stairs behind him. She wanted to cower behind him, but the platform was open on all sides so there was truly nowhere to hide. She stood there looking at her feet, hoping the world would just continue to move past her.

"Stop it," Harley told her, squeezing her hand. "Stand tall and proud. Face your destiny. This is what your mother and father sacrificed their world for. Whether you like it or not, be proud of your heritage. You are the daughter of a Gifted and a man who has served his country in every way he could."

This made Marra straighten her shoulders and look up. She smiled shyly at him. "Thank you."

"We all need a reminder every now and then." He winked at her. "If it helps, pretend they are all looking at me and wondering why on Segarris I am waiting here, rather than walking in, and where are my bodyguards."

Marra squared her shoulders. "You don't need bodyguards."

"You, my protective one, do have to sleep."

"Ah, yes, and now thanks to you I can actually sleep without nightmares. Though, I do worry you will never get a peaceful night's sleep again. I have been meaning to ask. How did you know to sing that song?"

"Your mother told me. It is a song your father would sing to her when she was overwhelmed with others' emotions and her senses were confused. The sweet lullaby would ease everything. They told me your nightmares may get worse in Segarris and how to help you."

"Look at you two up there, announcing to the world you are here. Do neither of you have common sense. Get down from there," an ancient male voice commanded.

Marra jumped in fright. She had been so caught up in the conversation with Harley that she had forgotten where they stood. Marra looked over to see a man with grey hair and wrinkled brown eyes glaring up at her. "I would know you anywhere. You did not need to wear the cape."

Marra instinctively tightened her hand on the feathered cloak. "Mother insisted," she attempted to explain. "She said it would make it easier for others to believe."

"I will always be guided by her." He inclined his head. "But I am certain she did not say walk into the Settlement and climb the platform for all to see."

"Well, no. That was not part of the instructions." Marra felt like she was back in school, being chastised by the headmaster.

Harley acted like none of the reprimand bothered him, which it probably didn't. He was a prince, and no one would be foolish enough to tell him off.

"And you, after going to all the trouble to hide your whereabouts, first announce where you were this morning with the incident in Aviggayillis and now standing on the platform for the world to see. Have you lost what little mind the Gods gave you?"

Marra almost laughed at Harley's face. It appeared being heir to the throne held no sway to this man.

She rushed down the stairs and stood before the old man. "I see you inherited your father's height." His voice softened. "And your mothers eyes. How are they both?"

He didn't wait for them but moved off into the city.

"They are well," Marra replied cautiously. She didn't know who this was and did not want to give away information she shouldn't.

"A council meeting is being hastily gathered to discuss your arrival and what it means. Many were warned this was coming but chose not to believe it, but here you are. To be admitted for training formalities must be observed. I brought your mother before the council, but this time my son will speak for you."

Everything fell into place. "You are Heiranni? You officiated my parents' Bonding?" Marra spoke quietly as they moved through the streets.

The brusque manner disappeared to be replaced by a warm smile. "It is nice to be remembered."

"She told me to do whatever you said."

"Always a clever one, that Kahlahnni."

"Your son is Lopakka?' Marra hoped she pronounced it correctly. "He was the first Pomaikkan mother ever spoke to."

"Yes. She has taught you much."

"I have only recently learned the truth. I am still grappling with things, to be honest."

"You are going to have to grapple later. We are here," Heiranni announced.

Marra walked out into what would be called a town square in medieval days, but this one held another raised wooden platform; though, it was higher and had large round pillars at each corner. There was a long table in the center of the platform and on one side sat four men and four women in clothing similar to Marra's. In front of the table stood a middle-aged man, waiting patiently, his hands clasped behind him. "And here they are," he announced loudly as they walked to the bottom of the stairs. "Prince Harlonngraith, would you please escort your guest to be presented to the council?"

"Thank you, Lopakka, it is my honor."

Harley led the way and Marra found herself standing between the two men. One towered over her, while she was several inches taller than the other. "Members of the council of Pomaikka, I am honored to introduce you to Lady Samarra Kahlahnni Cellecia Durrand."

There were several shocked looks from members of the council and whispering from the people who had gathered to witness the council meeting. "Lady Samarra, would you kindly show us your brand?" Lopakka asked.

"I was not branded like others of the Segarrin nation, but I do carry the markings in another form." Marra hesitated. Being the center of all this scrutiny was making her anxious and her hands shook at the thought of being judged by so many.

Harley took the feathered cloak from her. "Show them," he said. "Prove who you are."

With those words of encouragement, Marra rolled up her sleeves to reveal both the Warrior and Gifted tattoos. The whispering turned to cries of outrage, and she was now met with scowls from several people on the council. "You forget yourselves and your history good citizens of Ohanelle, Samarra, daughter of Kahlahnni, does not carry the marking of the Seer, she carries the marking of the Gifted. Samarra has been blessed by the Gods and you would all do well to remember it."

"How is this possible?" a woman sitting at the council table demanded.

"Yes, how?" a man two seats down from her joined in.

"Rather than being outraged, why don't we simply ask her?" Lopakka pointed out, cheerfully.

Marra had a suspicion that he was quite enjoying himself. She rolled her sleeves back down, completely self-conscious of everyone staring. What would they ask her? What could she possibly say that would make them welcome her? After all, why were they simply not welcoming her because of her parentage? Were they not all about protecting their own?

Lopakka turned to Marra and spread his hands wide. "Do you have a gift, Samarra Kahlahnni?" he asked loudly, so all in the open square could hear. It was clever of him to use her mother's name too.

"I don't think so," she said the words softly.

"Then why are you here with the Gifted brand upon your wrist?" he asked.

"To complete my training."

"Ah, yes, your training. But what training? By your mother's letter your Warrior training is complete, your father has done all he can, and you have earned your branding," Lopakka announced, taking a handwritten letter from the inside of his vest.

"I had it delivered while we waited at the first platform," Harley said under his breath.

Marra quickly realized that the exchange between Heiranni and Harley had all been for show, to give the letter time to arrive and be read by Lopakka. She nodded but said nothing.

Lopakka held the letter high. "The Seer Kahlahnni states that her daughter is gifted and needs training. Who here will question the word of the Seer?" The challenge hung in the air. He turned back to Marra, tucking the letter away. "Are you gifted, Samarra?"

"I don't think so." She stammered the words, her shyness coming through. A feeling of deja vu swept over her—of not fitting in and people staring. It took all her courage not to run. She got a lot of feelings of deja vu of late. *It's just your overactive imagination*, she dismissed the thoughts, *great for writing books, bad for standing in front of demanding strangers.*

"Would you be so kind as to roll up your sleeve and give me your wrist with the Gifted marking on it?" Marra did what she was told. He took her hand and with almost the same reverence that Harley had shown the first time he had seen it, Lopakka placed his hand over it. The tattoo grew warm. "I want you to look at me and only me." His voice was hypnotic and Marra did what was instructed. "Tell me," he continued.

A word floated to the surface of her thoughts. The word was the same as the one she had overheard her parents use, the one when she wasn't focused on her writing she would scribble over and over again on her page. It was a Pomaikkan word, but one she didn't know the meaning to.

"You are safe; you can say it," he urged.

Marra decided to trust her instincts as she did when she was sparring. They didn't fail her then and she hoped they wouldn't fail her now. "Moehanne." The word rang out across the square. There was complete silence. All sound ceased for a few seconds, and it was like Marra was stuck in a vacuum where she could hear nothing, but her own heartbeat.

The silence was shattered by a whoop from the grumpy council lady. "Two Gifts in my lifetime, we are certainly blessed."

"I take it that settles the issue?" Harley asked over the noise.

"Yes, there will be a council vote at some point to put in the records, but Samarra will begin her training tomorrow," Lopakka explained.

"I am sorry, but I do not understand," interrupted Marra. "What does Moehanne mean?"

"Soul Sleeper. It is not as powerful as your mothers, to be honest, but it certainly is useful if you know how to use it."

"Is that why I feel moments of having lived an experience before, because I am seeing what is to come?"

"Yes, that's exactly it."

Marra felt the blood drain from her face. This was not good. Not good at all. Her dreams were real! "I feel sick," she said softly, placing the back of her hand over her mouth.

Harley and Lopakka both looked worried. "I keep dreaming that Harley dies..." This got their attention. She could almost not bare to say the rest, but she forced it out. "He dies by my hand."

Chapter 18

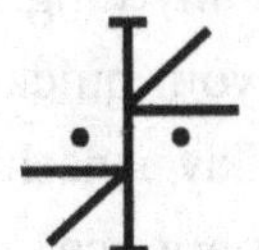

Harlonngraith

Marra's words kept repeating in his head. He banished them for the third time and redirected his focus back to the woman floating beside him. It had been a huge day for her. Neither of them had known this morning that by the evening meal she would know that the marking she had got to honor her mother was the symbol she would have been branded with if she had grown up in Segarris. "Please, try not to worry about it," he said, reaching out to massage her shoulders. "I am absolutely certain that you are not going to kill me."

"Really?" Her voice was small in the dimly lit private bath house. "Are you truly sure?"

"Do you think I would be sitting here with you all by myself if I thought there was a remote chance you were going to try to kill me?" He kept rubbing her shoulders. "Think about it. I am aware of how quickly you could end my life if the mood took you, and you have thrown a knife at me, and yet here I am, completely naked, exposed to you, without a bodyguard in sight."

"Are you ever not going to bring up that knife throwing thing?" Her voice was a little exasperated, which he took as a good sign and grinned behind her back.

"Well, I can't promise anything, but I will try to refrain from reminding you of your quick temper."

"Ha." She turned quickly, splashing water everywhere. "Says the man with no patience."

"No one is perfect," he said airily.

She reached out and traced his lips with her fingertip. "You are perfect to me."

Harlonngraith took her hand in his and kissed the palm and then raised her wrist out of the water and kissed her brand. It was the Warrior one. "How did I get so lucky?"

"I could say the same," she countered.

"Mmmm." He changed the subject before he put his foot in it and mentioned her being his Champion. "How do you feel about starting your training tomorrow?"

"Nervous, but also intrigued, with a touch of let's hope they can teach me to sleep without you having to sing to me every night."

"I like singing to you," he admitted.

"Yes, but you need your sleep too. How will you perform your princely duties if you can't think straight because you are too tired from singing to me all night?"

"Princely duties?" He laughed. "What princely duties do you speak of?"

Marra smiled at him. "There must be some fancy things only a prince can do to keep you occupied while I learn?"

"I'll worry about that tomorrow. For now, I am more interested in fulfilling other duties." He leered at her.

This made Marra laugh, which made his heart soar. The look of fear that had crossed her face when she had confided her dreams to him and Lopakka would not leave him anytime soon. All he cared about, for the moment, was making her feel safe and unafraid of what her dreams might bring. He wondered if Evan had done that for Lahnni when they first met.

"Your Highness?" There was a firm knock on the door.

Harlonngraith frowned. He had made it clear they did not want to be disturbed. "What?" he said crossly.

"There is a sergeant here for you. He says he has the reports and ledgers you required."

"Thank you. Get him something to eat. I will be there in half a turning."

Chapter 19

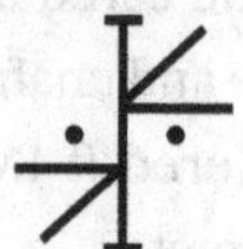

Harlonngraith

Prince Harlonngraith, first born son and heir to the throne of Segarris, was at a loss. He had been studying the ledgers the sergeant had brought and was finding many discrepancies, but he didn't truly understand what he was looking at. He wished his brother Platisse was here. Harlonngraith was certain his knowledge of the church was what was lacking in this situation. He just didn't know enough about the branding ceremony. To ease his annoyance at not being able to find anything useful, he had been working out with some of the men and women his age and who he had sparred against when he lived here years prior but was beating them all. He wanted to demand that they not worry about his title, but that would appear rude and petulant, so, in the end, he excused himself on the pretense of getting water.

The noise of giggling children drew him to another section of the large area set aside for training. Harlonngraith smiled to himself as he remembered his first day trying to get the kids to do what he asked. He missed those classes and working together with Samarra.

He walked around the corner and into the room he knew was set aside for training the younger ones. It was midmorning and he guessed this class had just come from other lessons where they had been sitting and concentrating. They were restless. Approximately twenty-five pairs of eyes turned to look at him. A young man stood at the front of the class, his hands on his hips, clearly losing his patience with the unruly class.

"Sorry to interrupt, Eltta." He recognized the man. They were about the same age and had had several classes together when Harlonngraith had been sent to study here. "The giggling drew me."

Eltta smiled warmly. "Class, this is Prince Harlonngraith, he will sit the throne one day and lead Segarris well. Say good morning."

The class responded with varying degrees of enthusiasm. "I am happy to meet you all." He kept his voice light and slightly higher pitched than normal. He knew how intimidating he could come across. "I was hoping Eltta wouldn't mind if I help teach you today?"

The look of surprise on Eltta's face was priceless. "Be my guest." He bowed to the prince. "Would you like to take the class or help with the class?"

"If I am not stepping on toes, I would like to take the class."

Eltta turned back to the class. "The prince is going to be in charge today. I don't think I need to tell you how disappointed your parents would be if you do not behave properly. If you have a question do not yell out, raise your hand and address him as Your Highness."

They all nodded, their little faces serious. "Thank you, Eltta." Harlonngraith knelt down on one knee. "Can you all gather around for a moment, please?"

They did what he asked. When they were mostly listening or at least looking in his direction, he spoke quietly. Having learned from Samarra that if you spoke softly they would try to hear you and concentrate better. "While we are out in the Settlement or if you ever meet me at court, you must call me Your Highness, but while I am your teacher you may call me Harley. It can be our little secret, okay?" he asked.

They all nodded. "Great." He grinned at them. "Now, I want you to run two laps around the room. And go!" He stood and made a shooing motion. Few children ever needed to be told twice that they were free to run, and soon everyone was laughing as they ran around the perimeter of the room.

The class went smoothly, and by the end of it Harlonngraith was sitting on the floor telling them about a princess he had met in a far off kingdom who could fight better than anyone he knew. He didn't know who was having a better time, the kids or himself. If their normal teacher, who came in to collect them, thought it odd to find the prince sitting amongst the children, with one little girl bold enough to have sat on his lap, they said nothing. He waved goodbye and promised he would come and teach them again soon.

When the room was quiet and it was just Eltta and himself, Harlonngraith stood and stretched. "Thank you for that. It was what I needed."

"I never thought I would say this, but you have a way with children."

"I just had a good teacher. Samarra is a brilliant instructor. I learned most of it from her."

"If it is not too forward of me to say, I think the Moehanne is good for you."

It was the first time Harlonngraith had heard someone call Samarra that and he fretted, though with his court training he didn't show it. It was another thing she had to adjust to, and he felt like all he had done was bring complication and confusion to her world. "Yes, she is very good for me."

"Well, I must be off. I have another class." Eltta held out his hand and Harlonngraith grasped his forearm. "I mean this when I say any time you are free please find me and help out. Wherever you have been training of late has improved your technique."

Harlonngraith smiled. "Thank you, I shall take you up on that offer. If it would not be an imposition, I will also be looking for someone to spar with every now and then and would like it if they didn't always let me win."

This made Eltta laugh. "You figured it out."

"Captain Evannderth pointed it out," Harlonngraith said sourly, making Eltta laugh harder.

"Is he as good as they say?"

"Yes, but I think his daughter is better."

Eltta whistled with appreciation. "Now, that is something I would like to see."

"I am sure she will be looking for opponents daily to spar with. Offer to be one. It will be a nice change for her to kick someone else's arse aside from mine."

"She has definitely changed you," Eltta repeated as he left the room.

Harlonngraith's smile slid from his face as he thought about Eltta's words. Samarra had changed him. She had made him a better person in many ways and what has he given her? The option to kill someone or give up her life for him, and if she didn't like those options she could just sit back and watch him die. The guilt he felt was heavy and growing daily as the date he needed to arrive at the Challenger's Arena was fast approaching. Which meant her answer was going to be required within the next week or two.

Samarra

"You need to relax. We have time." Lopakka tried to reassure her. "Your mother trained for several years to hone her skills. It's been a week and you are pushing yourself to know everything."

"You said mum's gifts were more complicated than mine. So, I shouldn't take as long to learn to understand and control them."

This made Lopakka laugh. "You need to cease that mindset immediately. Kahlahnni can only control her gifts to a degree, she cannot manipulate what she sees. It is more about letting in what she wants and understanding what is given her. This will be the same for you, just to a smaller extent. You will learn to remember your dreams and interpret them. And if you are gifted enough, you could possibly learn to hover in the place between, on the cusp between waking and sleeping, they are usually the ones of special importance. We have many dreams, big dreams, little dreams, wishing dreams. Learning to differentiate and still have restful sleep will take time to complete."

"I don't have that much time. Teach me what you can in two weeks, and after that I am leaving."

"Where do you go in such a hurry, may I ask?"

Marra looked at him and wished she knew the answer, but she was still torn. "A decision must be made and Harlonngraith must leave." She knew her response was cryptic, but that's all she could think to say.

Lopakka sat and looked at her. His big brown eyes thoughtful and concerned. He nodded. "Yes, he is cutting his time close to find..." Lopakka stopped and blinked at her. "Oh, you poor child. I wonder what our Gods are thinking at times. You carry both the Warrior and Gifted markings in plain sight, something even your father doesn't do. His Noble brand hidden from the world." Lopakka stood and walked around the small room they practiced in. "You are evenly balanced, like the scales both you and your mother see in visions and dreams. It is you, you are the scales, what you do decides it all. It is not whether Harlonngraith or Tommofey sit the throne, it is you and your choices that will tip the scales one way or another. That is why your mother cannot see more. Everything is so finely balanced."

Marra sat there watching him pace. "I am the scales?" She tried to make sense of his ramblings.

"Yes."

"What I am is more confused than ever," she confessed. "There is so much I don't understand."

Lopakka stopped walking and came to sit back down. "Yes, much has been kept from you, probably for your own good, knowing your parents. I do not know where you have been raised, but clearly it is not in Segarris."

Marra didn't respond to that because what was there to say, instead she tried to focus on things that would help her to move forward with this new power. "What I need to learn immediately is how to sleep without Harley having to sing to me all the time."

"He sings you to sleep?"

"Yes. Mother used to sing me to sleep when I was too scared to close my eyes because of the nightmares. Turns out that it works at keeping the emotions of others away from her too. Dad would sing it when they were in crowded areas—or hum it."

"Can you sing it for me?" Lopakka seemed truly fascinated.

Marra cleared her throat. She enjoyed singing but singing in front of people was something she loathed. Her voice was quiet and wobbly as she sang the first verse.

She stumbled slightly when Lopakka joined her in the chorus and sang the second verse and final chorus with her.

"Your father knew this song?"

"Yes, and Mum said that once he sang it she could recall the words but didn't know how. They thought it was a lullaby."

Lopakka nodded. "It is not a lullaby. It is an ancient hymn used in prayer. In essence when the prince sings it to you he is asking the Gods to protect you from ill omens."

"I wonder how my parents know it?"

"So do I. It is something I wish they were here to discuss."

Marra felt a sudden pang of homesickness. "I miss them very much. Things would be easier if they were here."

"Easier and more complicated, me thinks. This is about you and your time to grow. You would be overshadowed if they were here."

"But would I?" Marra screwed up her face to show her doubt. "I am the newly revealed Moehanne, and Prince Harlonngraith's Champion. Not sure they could trump that at the moment."

"So, you have accepted your fate?" he asked.

Marra stopped and thought about what he asked, and then the words she had just spoken sunk in. She had just admitted to another person that she was the Champion. "Do I have any choice?"

"There is always choice."

"I can't choose to walk away and let someone else fight in my stead. I am his best hope at living through this Challenge. I don't know if he is supposed to sit the throne, but I know I will be the one standing beside him in the Arena, ready to respond to anything the priests have in store. He is the love of my life and there is no point living without him, so I will die for him or live with him."

"I think you know him better than anyone. Do you think he will make a good king?"

"Yes." Marra straightened a little in her chair and looked him square in the face.

"Why?"

"Because he is willing to learn. He knows he doesn't know it all and he cares enough to want to learn to help others." She smiled as she remembered his first tea making efforts. He didn't need to learn it and it was a simple example but it was important. He understood that small things matter to people. He was also willing to be taught when she pointed out his fighting stance put him at risk, she did have to show him how, but after that he was more than willing to learn and accept her guidance.

"That is important in a leader." Lopakka took a sip of his wine and looked at her over the rim of his cup. "I think you might find your nightmares lessening for now."

Marra tried to figure out what he meant by that. "Why? You haven't taught me anything yet."

"No, but I think the dreams of you killing him will be gone now you have made your decision."

Understanding came to her. "I was dreaming that I was killing him because by not being his Champion, in my mind, I may as well have been plunging the knife into his heart myself."

Lopakka nodded.

"Still doesn't help me long term. I am sure new dreams will come soon."

"I have no doubt." He put down the wine and flexed his hands. "Because we don't have a lot of time, for now I will teach you to keep them at bay, on one condition." he held up his finger to her.

"Okay," she agreed hesitantly.

"Once the Challenge has been accepted, and if indeed you live, you must come back and complete your training. I want a six-month commitment from you. Do we have a deal?"

"Fine," she agreed with a huff.

"Good. Now let us begin in earnest. No more excuses from you."

Chapter 20

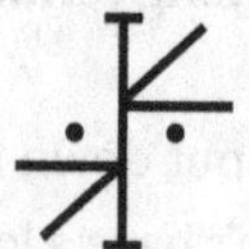

Harlonngraith

"You're toying with me," Harlonngraith complained as they circled each other in the main training area.

She grinned at him. "What makes you say that?"

"Because if you were home, you would have thrown me over your shoulder twice by now."

"I am not toying with you, I am saving your dignity," Samarra admitted. "There are a lot of people watching and I want them to see how much you have learned since the last time you were here."

"I appreciate that as the prince, but as your boyfriend I want everyone to see how incredible you are."

"Then we are at an impasse because I have no intention of making you look anything other than competent in front of everyone."

Harlonngraith stopped circling, stood still, and bowed to her. "Fine, then you can spar with someone else. It is time for them to see why you are able to wear the Warrior brand."

Samarra stepped in close and even though there were many people watching them and more gathering as word spread, it felt like they were completely alone. "I know why I wear the Warrior brand. I figured it out." She beamed up at him, and all he could do was remind himself not to kiss her here and now. It would undermine what he wanted to achieve.

"I'm listening." He smiled, not being able to resist returning her enthusiasm. She was in a fine mood today. It reminded him of simpler times, before he had brought his world into her life.

"I wear the Warrior brand because I am one, and I wear it on my wrist and not hidden, like most people who have a second symbol because I am unique."

"I know that."

"Yes, but you haven't asked why I am unique." She said the words lightly, as if playing a game.

He laughed. "Fine. Why are you unique?"

Before he could stop her, she reached up and caressed his face in front of everyone. "Because, my beloved, I am your Champion, and there has never been one like me."

Harlonngraith's mind froze, a wave of relief quickly followed by horror, and ending in guilt swept over him. Her words reverberated through his mind.

The smile slowly slid from her face. "Say something," she said anxiously.

"I'm sorry." No longer caring who witnessed his love for this woman he took her face between his hands and bent and kissed her tenderly. "I am so very sorry to have done this to you. You deserve more than that. You deserve the world, not a fight to the death."

Tears shone in her eyes, but she raised her head, clearly proud of who she was. "You allowed me to choose, and I choose you. But now I must prove it to everyone that I am the one."

He frowned. What did she mean by that? Samarra stepped out of his embrace and turned her back to him, instead facing the crowd that was watching them both with growing curiosity. They had accepted her as a Moehanne quickly, he hoped they would have no issue with her being his Champion.

"I issue a challenge. Bring forth your best fighters. The prince is easy to beat, and I want a contest," she joked.

"What are you doing?" he asked quietly.

"Proving myself, so I become the only choice by the time we leave."

"You are so damned clever." He admired her from behind.

"Why, thank you, my prince."

"Prince Harlonngraith says you are exceptional. Let's see you prove it." Eltta stepped forward.

Harlonngraith shrugged at Eltta. "I did warn you. Don't come to me when you are sore tomorrow." He moved back out of their way.

"Choose your weapon, Moehanne." Eltta deferred to Samarra with respect.

"Thank you for the offer, but I would rather have you choose yours."

Harlonngraith watched with admiration as Samarra did to Eltta what she had done to him the first time they had sparred. Now he could see how she pushed just far enough to assess and give a false sense of security before she pounced and completely dismantled your skills. Eltta landed on his knees with a grunt as she swept his legs out from under him. "Now, would you care to fight like you mean it?" Marra asked as she stepped back and allowed him to stand.

Eltta inclined his head. "You are the Moehanne," he tried to explain.

"At this moment, I am Prince Harlonngraith's Champion," she announced loudly. This brought a round of gasps, followed by a lot of talking, which she ignored. "I am here to prove I am the only candidate. Fight me properly or step aside."

"Is this true, Your Highness?" an older woman's voice interrupted Harlonngraith's viewing. He turned to find it was the same vocal council member they had encountered their first day when both of Samarra's markings had been revealed.

"Yes, Lady Samarra is my Champion." Harlonngraith always liked to use her title to remind people of who they were talking about. He was looking down at the old woman as well as trying to watch Samarra and Eltta.

"That is a lot to burden on one young woman."

Harlonngraith turned fully and stared at the Po-maikkan council member. "You make it sound like I had anything to do with the choice."

The woman looked a little flushed as if she finally understood to whom she addressed. "Your Highness, I did not mean to give offense."

"I can assure you the Lady is ready for any trial the Gods throw at her. Her parents have seen to that."

As if to prove his point, there was a thud and an enthusiastic round of applause which caused him to look up to find Eltta lying on his back, holding a hand to his cheek. Samarra looked to Harlonngraith who winked his encouragement before he raised his voice. "Anyone else like to test my Champion?"

Chapter 21

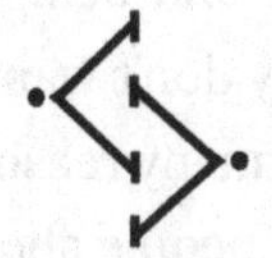

Samarra

Her dreams were mostly peaceful, a sash with symbols that blazed in the dark and red flowers everywhere seemed to be mostly what she remembered. Though, there was ever a feeling of being watched, like a shadow lurked in the corner, waiting for something. Marra was learning the very basics of what the term Moehanne meant and was grateful that her dreams of killing Harley had subsided. For now, it was about distinguishing her normal, average dreams from the other types and waking from ones she didn't want to experience before she would start to learn how to interpret them.

"How do you know so much about Gifts when there has been none for several generations?"

"My family have been entrusted to collect, record, and understand the gifts as much as we can for when these moments arrive. It has been an honor to work with you and Kahlahnni, and help you both with understanding what we have learned."

"Are there other types of Gifts?" she asked slowly. "Are you allowed to discuss them with me?"

"We can discuss Gifts in broad terms with any Po-maikkan. It is up to the one with the Gift to decide how much they disclose with others about their own abilities. From what I have read and being around Lahnni, most share the basics as they don't want others to know what is and isn't possible for many reasons. It will be up to you to decide what you tell people about what you can do."

Marra studied Lopakka and raised her eyebrows at him. "Do you not know the answer to my question or are you avoiding it?"

"When you have completed your training you will have access to our records, then you can discover the answer for yourself. We record all we do here for the future gen-erations, and our records are well-tended by my family. It is a privilege we are honored to hold."

"Did my mother look at the records?"

He frowned. "I actually don't know. I was out doing oth-er things at the end of her training. I had given up hope of her ever seeing me as anything other than a brother figure, so to heal my wounded heart, I went exploring for a while. Why do you ask?"

"You were in love with my Mum?" Marra didn't know why but it surprised her.

"Who wouldn't be? She is beautiful, kind, and tough. She had been through so much and yet was only more compassionate for it. I stupidly asked her to read me once, thinking it would reveal that we were destined to be together, she told me to seek my happiness through books and knowledge. I asked her if she saw us linked. She said yes, but couldn't see how, just that she trusted me with something more precious than her life. It was the most she ever saw of herself in a vision, she admitted."

Marra sat forward in her chair, no one spoke of her mother's gift and she was still in awe of it. "Was she right?"

Lopakka looked surprised. "You tell me."

"Hang on, am I missing something?"

"No, you just aren't looking at it the right way."

This made Marra stop. What was she not seeing? She thought about his words. He was surrounded by books and knowledge and appeared perfectly content with his life. She knew he was married and had two daughters who were only a few years younger than herself. Where was the link to her mother in that? Then it hit her and Marra blinked rapidly as if processing the idea more. "I'm the link. I'm the thing more precious than her life."

"Yes. When she saw me, she saw you needing me, and I am honored to make that vision come to fruition for the Seer."

Samarra

"Pizza," Marra announced to the assembled children. "The prince and I are making pizza and I need some helpers. Does anyone want to help?" All but a few of the shyer children raised their hands or yelled enthusiastically. Marra smiled at as many as possible as they crowded around her. "Wonderful, but first you must wash your hands."

She had had rows and rows of tables brought out and set up in front of the large wooden platform that sat in the center of the city. The tables held bags of flour, flat bowls of salt, and jugs of fresh water. Larger bowls of a delicious, thick passata which would serve well as a base. Beautiful fresh white, soft cheese bobbed in ceramic jars of milky liquid, similar to buffalo mozarella back home, and an assortment of toppings already chopped and ready to be added were laid out on large platters. Hot stones for roasting were set up around the tables, enough for each child to not have to share. It had been a massive effort to have all of this sourced, assembled, and set up, but before she left, Marra wanted the children who hadn't been lucky enough to be taught by Harley the chance to spend time with their prince.

Marra hummed softly to herself as she watched the children line up in front of Harley, who was in charge of hand washing inspection at the water pump nearby. Eltta stood with her, the area around his eye a lovely shade of yellow, almost healed from their last round of sparing. Marra sported two bruises from the encounter on her thigh. He was good.

"You both make me sick, you know," Eltta commented wryly.

Marra stopped humming and turned to the man who was quickly becoming a good friend. "Who makes you sick?"

"You and your prince."

She tried to stop her smile but failed. "Um, thanks."

"Both of you carry so much responsibility and yet you make everything seem effortless. What is your secret?"

"If only you knew just how much is a charade." Marra looked over to the man who she was going to fight for... literally. "He has been trained his entire life to look serene, in control, and competent, regardless of what he is facing. No one wants a ruler who will fall apart at the first moment of difficulty. He hides his fears and faults better than most, that is all."

Eltta nodded. "Well, that makes it far less romantic and more pragmatic."

"Pragmatic is the only way we survive this," she said quietly. "He is the prince, heir to the throne, don't get carried away with the fairytale."

This earned her a sharp look from Eltta. "He has changed, he was never arrogant, but there was an air to him that is no longer. He is more open to people, less guarded. His mother has made him wary of everyone."

Marra agreed. "He has changed for the better, but that was his doing, not mine. He just needed someone to see him. I will always love him, but after my duty as Champion is fulfilled and we both live, I have committed to return here and he will no doubt go home and become King and do all the kingly things that need doing, like marrying some princess and producing heirs."

"You say it so calmly," Eltta noted, reaching out and touching her arm in comfort.

"I am content here and now. I am living for the moment. My life has become beyond complicated and all I can do is enjoy the now. Wherever I am, I need to be good with that or I fear I might go crazy."

"Easier said than done," commented Eltta.

Marra felt sadness begin to creep in but refused to wallow in it. She had much to be happy about, and she needed to be mindful of the positive. Her mother had taught her that. You can either take in negative energy or positive energy, and it has a profounder affect than most would know. Combined with her father's discipline to concentrate solely on what was in front of you when you sparred, because as soon as the mind wandered you would lose, these were her two greatest abilities. Looking at the positive and concentrating on what was in front of you.

"Ha, everything is easier said than done. If it wasn't, the world would be full of accomplished people rather than people sitting and not doing and waiting for someone to provide their happiness."

"I fear that is the default mode of most."

Marra shrugged. "I wish everyone happiness, but I will never understand the ones who complain about it but never change."

Their discussion was ended by the first children returning to her, hands held high to prove they had washed as instructed. Marra turned to Eltta. "My friend, I have enjoyed the chat, but duty calls. Are the fires ready?"

"Yes, I have several parents at each fire pit ready to help. I think we have it under control. I can't wait to taste this thing called pizza."

"Thank you. I will make a few for all the helpers to enjoy once the children are fed."

"Great." Eltta pointed to a roaring fire with several people standing around it. "Send the first mob that way."

"Will do."

The next turning was spent teaching the children to make dough, and while it rested, they played several games and she taught them all to respond when she clapped a certain pattern at them. Then it was back to the dough, rolling it out, and shaping it into a flat circle. As Marra moved from table to table explaining what to do, Harley moved amongst the children helping when their little hands couldn't reach what was required in the middle of the table. He tickled them and played silly games, like tapping them on the shoulder and pretending to hide behind another child while his hulking form could clearly be seen. Marra's heart was light and she couldn't remember a time where her world felt more complete. She didn't think about tomorrow or the coming battle, she simply marveled in the joyous and innocent fun of the moment.

Marra caught Harley whispering to several children and there was much pointing in her direction, though she pretended not to see anything. As she bent to help one of the boys who was getting upset that his circle was too square shaped for his liking, she kept an eye on the giggling children and her conspiring lover. What were they up to?

By the time she had the young boy calm and his base resembling more of a plate than a brick, Harley had snuck up behind her. She kept up the pretense of not knowing what was happening and felt a light tap on her left shoulder. Quickly she moved her head in mock surprise. "Who was that?" she asked the children as she turned back to face them. Before anyone could answer, she felt a tap on her right shoulder and with a fake worried expression turned to her right only to find Harley standing there grinning and without warning bent down and gave her a loud kiss, before quickly moving away. This made everyone at the table laugh, and Marra joined in. Harley tried to come in for a second kiss but this time she ducked and all he got was air, making the children laugh harder.

"Hey, no fair," he cried as he stomped his foot. But he was a little closer to the table than he thought and knocked it with his knee sending a bag of flour over the edge.

This made the children go silent to see how much trouble the prince would be in for having dropped the flour because he was being silly. Marra crouched down to pick up the broken bag. "Can someone please go and ask Eltta to get a broom?" she spoke, making sure her voice did not sound cross. She looked to find a crowd of little faces watching her. "It's okay, it was an accident," she assured them. But they just stood there, wide-eyed as if anticipating something. It was only then did Marra register that she didn't know where Harley had gone. She realized the children weren't watching her, they were looking over her shoulder. She turned to find Harley kneeling on one knee, holding out a black sash with symbols embroidered on the end she could see in a beautiful shimmering ice blue thread. "Will you be my Bonded?"

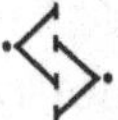

Harlonngraith

Samarra's gorgeous brown eyes looked up at him in wonder. "Bonded?" she repeated his word to back to him.

Harlonngraith reached out and wiped the flour from her forehead. "Yes, be mine. Let's ask Heiranni to perform the bonding ceremony just as he did for your parents."

"Um, wow." She sat down in the midst of the laughing and chatting children, the broken flour bag forgotten.

"Have you never thought about our future? What happens after you win in the Arena?" He sat down opposite her, tucking his legs in as best as he could.

"If I win," Samarra corrected.

Harlonngraith grew serious. He needed her to know that he wasn't being impulsive or frivolous; he had been thinking about this for a long time. "Okay, let me say this. I want to be Bonded to you now. I want to have that with you, to know we are connected in every way as you stand in that Arena, regardless of the outcome. If we die that day, then we die Bonded for all eternity."

Samarra nodded slowly and he took her hand. "I have thought about marrying you, I won't deny it." She paused.

"But?" he prompted.

"I never saw the point in following that daydream to its conclusion. It only leads to heartache."

This alarmed Harlonngraith. His heart pounded and his stomach constricted. What did she mean? Did she not love him like he loved her? "I want you with me, always."

"Harlonngraith, I was not raised to be a queen." Her voice was quiet. "I know nothing of your customs and..." She stopped, looking around. "I don't think this is the place to discuss this."

Children were trying to get their attention. "Lady Samarra." The little boy she had helped earlier pushed his way to the front of the gathered group. "I think you would make a very pretty queen," he announced proudly.

"Thank you, but there is more to being a queen than looking pretty."

An older girl, probably about ten, rolled her eyes. "We know that. You have to be clever too."

"I think you have to care about other people and help them," an older boy added.

"And I think Lady Samarra does all of those things." Harlonngraith spoke up. He was in awe of how the children saw directly to the heart of the matter.

"But you all forget one thing." Samarra spoke quietly, forcing the children to settle and be still to hear her. "Prince Harlonngraith, as set out in the accords, must marry a noble from a certain province." She turned to look him full in the face, a challenge in her brown eyes. "What province was that again?" she asked.

"Maybe we should discuss this later?" He looked around. "I am hungry. Who else is hungry? I think we need to get these pizzas made." Harlonngraith untucked his legs and pretended to struggle to get up so several children had to help him. This made everyone laugh and took the focus off Samarra. He tucked the black sash into the inside pocket of his vest and avoided making eye contact with her.

Harlonngraith

They were both quiet as they walked into their room later that night. He undid his boots and sat on the bed to take them off. She sat on a chair on the other side of the room to remove her boots. He frowned at the distance between them, trying not to read too much into it. Harlonngraith reached into his inside vest pocket and drew out the sash he had arranged with Heiranni to have hand crafted the first week they arrived at the Settlement. He placed it on the bed beside him, resting his hand on the Warrior and Gifted Symbols that were embroidered on it in his personal color of ice blue.

The silence drew out until it was unbearable. "What is it? You don't love me or don't want to be with me?"

He tried to keep the pain and fear from his voice, but it got caught in his throat. He swallowed hard and he told himself to get it together. Princes don't cry.

Samarra's perfect face watched him with growing wonder. "You are willing to risk the stability of your nation just to be bonded to me? Isn't that just as selfish as what your father did? Has your family not made enough poor choices?" she asked pointedly.

He moved quickly off the bed and came to kneel before her. "This is not just when we are talking about bonding. I promise I have thought this through, and though I want you for purely selfish reasons, I can see many reasons why bonding with you would be good for Segarris and its people."

"Are you not hearing me?" She stood and blew out her breath, her voice shaking. "You are supposed to marry someone else."

"That someone is not chosen yet. There is no woman sitting waiting for me to survive the coming Challenge. There is no one noble family who will be slighted if I back out of an agreement." Harlonngraith stood and took her shoulders, forcing her to look at him. "I want to change things. I want to move forward. I want to write new accords and I want to banish this need to fight for the right to rule." He looked at her pleadingly. "But I can't do that until you win for me."

"You want to write new accords?" she asked in a calmer tone.

"Yes, and I need a woman with strong morals and a different outlook by my side to do it. You make me think differently and the monarchy needs it. Segarris needs it." He hoped he was getting through. "I need it. I need you."

"I need you, too." Samarra's lip trembled as she said it. She reached out and wiped the tear that had slid down his face without him even realizing it.

"Be my bonded. Be my Bonded for the good of everyone or just because you love me, but please say yes." Harlonngraith kissed her. His lips soft as they brushed against hers. "Please," he whispered, kissing her again.

Samarra pulled back her head and looked up at him. "And it wouldn't hurt to have a Soul Sleeper, and a mother-in-law who just happens to be a powerful Seer, in your court," she pointed out.

He did not rise to the bait. "At this moment, all I care about is having you Bonded to my heart forever. Not the Champion to the Prince, or the Moehanne to the King, just you to me."

"Good answer."

Chapter 22

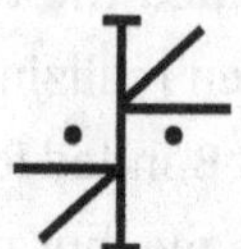

Harlonngraith

"Why do you not look happy?"

"I am happy."

"You do not look happy, you look worried," he insisted. "We are newly Bonded, you should be thinking carnal thoughts." He grinned wickedly.

"I am tired, nervous, anxious. There are so many things going on in my head."

"This night..." He was about to say is supposed to be special and realized just how much pressure she was under to be everything to everyone. He sat down next to Samarra on the bed and took her hand. "I am sorry. I wanted this to be perfect and I am making it not perfect," he apologized. He changed topics completely, an idea forming that would hopefully help her relax. "You know what I miss about your home?"

She shook her head. "No, what?"

"Endless hot showers. And it being just the two of us. No titles, no pressures, no expectations. Just Harley and Marra."

She shrugged, as if she didn't want to comment.

"Go on, you can say it. We are Bonded now, say whatever it is you want, you can't get rid of me now," he joked.

"I miss my parents' private garden, my anonymity, my parents, and endless hot water." She ended with a wink that eased his worries and made him smile.

"I did enjoy not being the prince for that first month, just being Harley and teaching beside you," he admitted. "I can't bring your parents here, but I think I can help with the other two." Harlonngraith reached up and ran his thumb across her lips. "I will have a private sanctuary built for you in the royal gardens, you will be the only one allowed to enter. It will have a pond, a bench, a tree, a statue, and of course a target to throw your daggers at rather than me," he promised cheekily.

She smacked playfully on his leg. "It sounds perfect," she sighed wistfully. Samarra looked a little less strained. "And the second thing?" she prompted.

"I don't know if you remember but when we were on the boat and packing to leave you said that you wished for a place to take a long soak?"

"I sort of remember you telling me to be careful what I wished for." She frowned at him. "We have been here for over a month and have had many soaks."

"Yes, in our private bathing room, but there is another place that you have not been to that I was thinking of when you said you wished to soak."

"Why have I not been there? Am I not allowed?"

Harlonngraith laughed. She was quick to forget the power and influence she now commanded. "You are my Champion and branded Gifted. You are now my Bonded, there is nowhere in this country you cannot go." He stood abruptly pulling her to her feet as he did so. "Take off that fine clothing and put on your robe," he ordered.

He strode to the door and opened it, finding two people standing there. One was there to protect them, though everyone by now knew that Samarra was capable of that, but as he had pointed out before, she had to sleep, and now with her gift being revealed, she was expected to sleep. The other person was there to help in any capacity he needed. They would fetch water, food, people, anything he required. They were in essence a Servant but with a Roamer brand. "I want the caverns cleared," he addressed the young man.

The thin man looked at him as if trying to register what he was asking. "All of them?"

"Yes, all of them."

"Now?"

Harlonngraith ground out the word, "Yes."

He stepped back into the room and closed the door, resisting the temptation to slam it. Harlonngraith chose to shake off the conversation and remind himself that the young man was probably not aware it wasn't a good idea to question the orders of a man who would be his king. Harlonngraith's thoughts were in several places, and he wanted to focus on Samarra and their first night as a Bonded couple, but something nagged at the edge of his mind. He hurried to his writing table and tore off a piece of parchment and took up a quill, uncorking the ink and quickly dipping it in, he didn't care if he made a mess, the note was for him alone. Why do Roamers have no other branding, yet they have all the castes within their society? He scrawled on the sheet before waving it around several times to let it dry, and then shoving it in the front of the Branding ledger he was still trying to understand.

"What are you doing?" Samarra asked from the other side of the room where she was tying up her robe, having done what he asked.

"I had a thought and didn't want to lose it." He turned to her and grinned wolfishly. "Now, I get to focus all my attention on you."

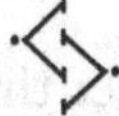

Harlonngraith

They stood at the bottom of a wide set of stairs that you entered from a small building on the far side of the Settlement, well away from the river and close to the drier lands that no one occupied. "Is it done?" Harlonngraith asked as he approached two men waiting at the bottom of the steps. One of them was Eltta.

"I was just about to have myself a nice soak, but yes, it is done," he complained, but his tone was light.

"I promise to make it up to you."

"Fine, you come and teach another class before you leave and we are even."

"Are you bribing your prince?" Harlonngraith feigned shock. He liked this feeling, it felt like Eltta could be his friend. Before Samarra he had never had friends.

"Never," Eltta winked. "And as a gift to you, my friends, I am going to have a chair brought down and guard this door myself."

"I am certain someone else can do that," Samarra said. "We have disturbed your plans already."

"Nonsense. It is a simple thing I do for my future king and queen."

Harlonngraith was not going to stand and argue with the man, he had more pressing things he wanted to do. "Thank you, Eltta. He held out his hand to his Bonded. "My Lady?"

She took it and he led her through a set of heavy, iron doors into a large antechamber where there were low benches along each wall, many crates sat on the benches and there were pegs evenly spaced around the walls. "What is this place?"

"The public bath houses of the Pomaikka. This part of the city is over a hot spring that feeds several large pools of water. The deeper we go into the cavern the hotter the water. There are five springs in total. The two hottest ones are much smaller."

"And why have we not bathed here before?" She looked around.

"It would be unseemly."

She frowned at him. "Why?"

"Because they bathe naked."

"Oh." She looked at him for a moment and then looked away. "Yes, probably not a good idea to have the heir parading around naked, putting the rest of the men to shame." Samarra looked up at him coyly.

Harlonngraith liked it when she shook off her shy moments and the flirty vixen came out. "I ordered everyone gone. We will not be disturbed, no one can hear us, and I plan to see just how well your high-pitched moans carry in here." He kissed her, savoring the sweet taste of her full lips.

"You ordered everyone out?" She sounded surprised. "Can you do that?"

"You do know you can do that too now?" He smirked and helped her out of her feather cloak, putting it safely on a hook before removing his own heavy cloak. Samarra slipped off her boots and so did he, placing them in a crate and putting them under the bench. She stood there in her pale red robe and he wore a pair of breeches. Harlonngraith pulled her into the first bathing area.

Samarra stopped and looked around. "I wouldn't do that," she replied absently resuming their conversation. "I don't think I will ever feel comfortable ordering people around like that."

"Neither would I, normally." Harlonngraith kissed her again, he couldn't seem to get enough of her. "Have you ever seen me order people like that before?"

Samarra cocked her head to one side, like she always did when she was thinking. "No, not like that."

"Like what?"

"Just because you can, purely for your wants."

He lifted her chin with his finger. "I order you around simply for my wants," he pointed out. Harlonngraith kissed her hard.

"That's different and you know it," she stated as they broke apart.

"Would you like to test the water?" He drew her over to the edge of the blue tiled pool. There were a few steps leading down into it. More benches and pegs lined the walls.

She walked over to the side of the pool and dipped her foot into it. "It's pleasant but will feel tepid quickly."

They did this twice more before Samarra settled on the fourth pool. Rather than the long rectangle shapes of the other three this pool was round, its tiles a dusky pink and from what Harlonngraith could see a ledge ran around the entire inside rim. The room was smaller than the other three and a sheet of steam hovered over the surface of the still water.

He undid the cord on his breeches and took them off, hanging them on one of the hooks. He held out his hand and Samarra handed him her robe. She didn't wait for him but walked to the round bath and stepped down onto the ledge. The water came up to her mid-thigh, she then took the next step down and the water sat at her waistline. When Harlonngraith stood beside her, it barely covered his pelvic bone, but then he considered that most of the Pomaikka were much shorter and the water would sit a lot higher for them.

Slowly and with a deep sigh of relief, he sank into the almost too hot water. Samarra mirrored his movement and the sound of contentment.

"This was a magnificent idea," she spoke quietly, as if not wanting to disturb the peace.

"I have them occasionally, but don't get too used to it. We have nothing like this at the palace."

Samarra floated closer to him and reached up to put her arms around his neck. "I'm sure you—" She stopped mid-sentence.

Harlonngraith opened his mouth to ask what was wrong when she put a single finger to her lips as well as covering his mouth with her other hand to indicate he shouldn't talk. She shook her head once, her usually beautiful brown eyes hard and focused, making his adrenaline pulse through him and he nodded in understanding. They were not alone.

Samarra

There was the faintest of sounds, a mere whisper of fabric that had alerted Marra, but it was enough to trigger everything her father had taught her. Harley went to speak but she put a finger to her lips as well as his to indicate he shouldn't talk. She shook her head once. She watched his eyes widen with understanding. They were not alone.

Marra stood and looked around, she couldn't see anything. "You said there is one more pool?" she asked loudly.

"Yes."

"I would like to see how hot it is," she announced and walked to the edge of the pool, closer to the last cavern and away from the open doorway to the others. None of the chambers had doors, just large arches that led into each room.

Marra didn't wait to see if Harley was coming, she knew he would follow. Keeping herself alert to any sound, she moved quickly to the next chamber and hurried through the arch. She looked around the small cave-like chamber. The pool was small, only being able to fit about ten people in it at any one time was her best guess. It was hard to determine, other than a light shade, what color tiles it had as the steam in the room was thick. It made the floor slippery and the humidity made her breathing more labored than normal. It reminded her of a sauna. She hated saunas.

Another scraping of sound was all the warning she got that someone was still approaching. Marra indicated to Harley for him to move to the right of the open archway while she headed for the small pool. She was naked and rather than try and hide it she would use it to her advantage. With care not to slip she stepped down onto the ledge that ran around the edge, where people would normally sit. She bent down and placed her hand in the hot water. Her feet and lower legs were protesting at the temperature, but she shut off that part of her brain.

In a few more seconds, a figure dressed in black, including a face wrapping, stood in the doorway of the room. She saw the shadow of another person behind him. "Hi," she said coyly, dragging her left hand through the water. "The prince seems to have left me alone, which one of you wants to join me?" She swore under her breath as she saw a third figure.

The first person walked into the small room, his eyes never leaving her body, cupping her hand, Marra threw the hot water at him, making him, and the person behind him, instinctively raise their arms to protect their eyes and stop moving forward. The third person halted before he could get into the room.

Marra stepped one leg out of the pool and grabbed the front of the intruder's top, pulling backwards. Her foot that was still in the water braced against the wall, and she used all her strength to propel the man over her and into the pool. As he hit the water, she stepped out of it completely and engaged the second man, noting that Harley had raised his fist to punch the next one stepping through.

Keeping the fact that the floor was slippery firmly in the forefront of her mind, Marra kept her steps small and didn't try to kick out quickly. She could lose her footing easily that way. The man in front of her was about her height with similar build, and was holding his dagger in a way that clearly told all that he knew how to use it. He recovered quickly from her throwing the water and circled away from Harlonngraith and toward the back of the room. Instead of following him, Marra moved to the opposite side of the doorway and put her back to it. That way they couldn't rush her, and she would know if another person came in. It was also too small a space for more than two of them to engage with her at any time without the risk of getting caught up with Harley and his opponent.

She heard a grunt and thud as someone hit the wall, without moving her head too much, Marra saw Harley holding his nose, blood dripping from his hand, his eyes angry. She had no more time to worry about her Bonded as the first person climbed out of the pool and rushed her, while the one that had tried to get her to the back of the room had returned and was also coming toward her.

Her training took over and Marra stopped thinking. She didn't consider the cold, or Harley, or being naked in front of strangers, her world became hyper-focused and it felt like it had sped up and slowed down in the same instant. Marra ducked and weaved; she lashed out and punched. While the men were decent fighters, they were clearly not trained to fight side by side in tight quarters and Marra took advantage of that by forcing them into each other's way as often as possible. As the one with the blade came at her, she stepped to the side and he followed her. He went crashing into his accomplice and it was all the opening Marra needed. She punched him in the throat and as he bent over and grappled for breath, she grabbed his blade and kicked him in the knee making him stumble backwards and into the pool. The one that was already soaked from his original fall into the pool was slightly taller than her and had a longer reach. His eyes were blood red and angry.

After a few more attempts to engage her, he became inpatient, which was what she had been waiting for and he overstepped. Marra ducked under his high swing and brought the knife across his throat in a smooth horizontal motion. She went to step out of his way as he stumbled backward but he grabbed her hair and pulled her with him into the pool.

Marra hit the water sideways and felt her rib cage connect with the ledge, but she took no notice. The grip on her hair loosened and she managed to get herself free. She stood and noticed the man now floating on his stomach, the water around him turning red. The man who she had punched in the throat, and she could almost guarantee had a broken knee cap, had been climbing back out of the pool when she had fallen in. He turned back but was not quick enough. The knife had left her hand before she even registered the decision. He fell half out of the pool, his hand coming up to clutch the knife now sticking out of his chest.

She didn't stop to think about the carnage around her, instead she looked to find Harley lying on the ground, his arms raised as the third assassin raised his boot to kick him in the face. Marra roared and heaved herself out of the pool, launching herself onto the attacker's back as his boot connected with Harley. Thankfully, he had managed to get his hand up to protect his face. Marra heard something crack and assumed it was a bone in her

Bonded's hand. Her mind snapped and she clung to the back of the black clad man. She wrapped her arm around his neck, tightly under his chin, and put him in a sleeper hold that cage fighters in her world used all the time. As he struggled to breathe and fought to remain conscious, she started to walk backwards dragging him with her. As he lost consciousness, she stepped backward into the pool, her mind blank other than knowing that he was the last of her enemies. She stepped off the ledge and into the center of the hot water, not registering the dead man floating next to them. Marra dropped to her knees, but did not let the man go; instead, she pulled his head under the water and there she stayed.

"Samarra?" She heard a voice call as if from far away. It sounded familiar. "Samarra, you have to let him go." The voice told her.

In a rush, everything came back and she let go of the man she was holding underwater. Without looking back, she crawled out of the pool, only now registering that her ribs really hurt. "Harley, are you okay?"

He was trying to prop himself up against the wall while cradling his hand to his chest. "I think I have a few broken fingers, and a twisted ankle." He made a face as she touched the swollen limb. "I slipped when we were fighting, that's how I ended up almost getting my head kicked in."

She stopped herself from touching his clearly broken nose. "I'll go get help."

"If you help me up, I would appreciate it. I don't want to sit here with them."

Marra looked over at the bodies of the three men she had just killed and with an odd detachment realized she felt no regret. No remorse, just an overbearing anger that they had dared to harm her or Harley. Was there something wrong with her? She would have liked to talk to her father about this, perhaps he could understand her lack of emotion.

"It turns out we did learn something from this," she said, her voice dull.

"What is that?" his voice was soft, gentle.

"I can kill without hesitation when required."

Chapter 23

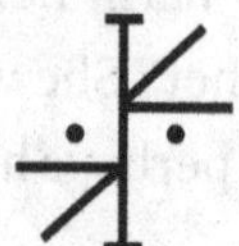

Harlonngraith

After having his freedom for five months Harlonngraith had found the return of his bodyguards restrictive. As they had made the trek across Central Seggar and into the forest of Saffed, to arrive at the almost forgotten Arena Harlonngraith had longed for nothing but the private moments he had at night with his Bonded.

On the second night after they had begun their journey to the Challenger's Arena, after having postponed their departure to stay for the funeral of Eltta, who had been killed the night the assassins had come for Samarra and himself. Though they were still unsure who the intended target was, Eltta had bravely fought off the four attackers, killing one while the others had slipped into the caverns. Samarra woke with a start, crying out in her sleep, and a guard rushed in, almost ending up with a knife in his heart. Thankfully, she managed to change her aim at the last minute and it embedded itself in the material of the tent wall instead. "Never come in here without being summoned."

The soldier had nodded his head and apologized. "We have been ordered to protect you."

"Yes, but who will protect you against my Bonded if you startle her? I think she has proven herself enough for you to know that if she needed help, she would call for it."

"There was a cry," he stammered.

Harlonngraith arched his eyebrow at the man, as if to say that there could have been several reasons why she had cried out. This time the soldier blushed and bowed out without trying to explain himself further.

Samarra had sat in bed, the blanket pulled up to her chin, staring blankly into space throughout the whole exchange. "Sorry for almost killing the guard."

"Would have been his own stupid fault." Harley moved slowly to sit himself up. His ankle was strapped, and several fingers had been put into splints to keep them straight while they healed. He had two black eyes and his nose was still too swollen to see if it would have to be re-broken to straighten. "What were you dreaming?" he asked as she cuddled against him.

"Red flowers."

"Red flowers?"

"Yes, several nights before you asked me to be Bond with you, I dreamed of the bonding sash wound around red flowers," she tried to explain.

"And you now just figured out what the red flowers meant?" he surmised.

"Yes. They were at Eltta's funeral. On his pyre and wound around the columns on the center platform."

"And you think they represent..." He wanted to make sure they were talking about the same thing.

"I think they are a warning of death. Maybe unexpected death?"

He was quiet as he let the words sink in. "I don't know if it would make a difference to know that."

"Eltta might be alive if I had known that red flowers are a warning of death." Her voice was full of anguish and all Harlonngraith wanted to do was take her pain away. He had kissed her forehead and held her while she cried. "I miss him too," was all he had said.

Now they had arrived at the Arena, the day before the Challenge was to be issued, and had just received word that Queen Anzhellika would be arriving by the evening meal. Preparations were being made to host the queen and her entourage, which Harlonngraith was happy to learn included his brother, Platisse and Arch Deacon Zussya.

"You look beautiful," he said as Samarra moved out from behind the changing screen.

She gave him a tight smile as she smoothed the soft folds of the ice blue dress over her hips. "Thanks. I hope your mother likes it."

Harlonngraith watched her closely. He noted the sadness that still touched her chocolate brown eyes...oh, how he missed chocolate. He almost laughed at his errant thought. He reached out and carefully tucked a few stray hairs that had escaped the knot of hair she had twisted on top of her head behind her ear. "You need to remember that for all my mother's blustering and ordering about, she is the Queen Regent, not the Queen."

"What do you mean by that?"

"She has only been the Queen Regent for this long because of this issue with me not being named heir by my father before he died, thus allowing Tom and Darria to challenge my right to rule. She makes no decisions for the nation and holds no vote in council once I reached my majority. Until I am king, my vote holds the same value as any other council member," he tried to explain succinctly.

"And once you are king?" she asked as she swung her arms in slow wide circles.

"Once I am king, if I choose, I can veto any vote and do what I want. My council in essence becomes advisory only." He watched her swing her arms. "What are you doing?" Harlonngraith asked.

Samarra gave him a rueful smile and dropped her arms. "Making sure I can fight if I need to."

"We are in the middle of a substantial company of soldiers. No one is getting close to us," he assured her. Since the assassination attempt, the two of them had been surrounded by bodyguards day and night.

"Your Highness," a voice called from the other side of the tent flap.

"Yes?" Harlonngraith answered without moving.

"Queen Anzhellika and Prince Platisse are here to see you."

Harlonngraith gave Samarra a peck on the cheek "Remember who you are and don't let them intimidate you," he said quietly. He knew her well enough now that he could see her shyness assert itself. It didn't matter what she accomplished or how many titles she had, until she felt comfortable around someone she was naturally shy, and him trying to force it would make it worse. "Let them in," he called out.

The flap was immediately pulled aside, allowing the late afternoon sun to come through. A tall woman, with long blonde hair, and perfect posture entered, followed by a man a few inches shorter than Harlonngarith and a few pounds heavier. He wore the cassock of a Brother of the Order of Seggar, with a simple cord around his waist rather than the fancier tasseled one like Arch Deacon Zussya. "Be welcome," he said in greeting before he embraced his mother and brother.

"It is good to see," Platisse spoke. "It has been too long."

"I am glad you came," Harlonngraith said with sincerity. If today was going to be his last evening meal he wanted to spend it with his family.

Queen Anzhellika moved to stand before Samarra, they were similar in height, but that was where it ended. "And this is the one you have set the country on fire for?" she asked as she stood back and eyed his Bonded up and down. "The gossip mongers speak of many things about this one."

Harlonngraith interposed himself between his Bonded and his mother, shocked at his mother's coolness. But should he be? It was only now that Harlonngraith recognized that Anzhellika was looking at Samarra as a rival for his affection, rather than an ally who would protect her son from all harm. "May I introduce you both to Lady

Samarra Kahlahnni Cellecia Durrand, my Champion and my Bonded." He moved to Samarra's side.

Prince Platisse bowed deeply to Samarra. "There are so many things I want to say and know, but first and foremost, welcome to the family."

"So, it's true. You Bonded with her." His mother raised a blonde eyebrow at them. "Well, I am sure we can spin it right. After all, we have never had a Roamer in the family, and it will tie them closer to the crown. There will, of course, have to be a proper royal wedding, a pagan ritual will never do for the King of Segarris. You have slighted an entire province, and that will have to be remedied in other ways too. Perhaps your brother, now you are both grown and safe from the machinations of my sister, could stop this nonsense about being a priest and come back to the palace and marry someone from Jaggiron?" Her voice grew gleeful as she looked over at Prince Platisse. "You could have the old palace. Once the bastard is killed, my sister can be thrown out of the palace and on to the street for all I care."

"Mother, stop," urged Harlonngraith. "Politics can wait, this may be Samarra's and my last day and I want to spend it with loved ones."

She seemed to not even hear him. "There are also whispers of her parentage. Is it true?" Queen Anzhellika finally looked Samarra fully in the face. "Are you the daughter of the Seer? And there seems to be some discussion that you carry different Gifts to your mothers?"

Harlonngraith felt queasy. This had not gone how he wanted it to at all. His mother appeared to only care about one thing and it wasn't him or Samarra. How had he not seen it before? Was this how Evannderth felt when he had Bonded with Kahlahnni? That he would risk it all to protect the woman he loved from the demands of a queen hell bent on power and revenge. Could Harlonngraith possibly still walk away from it all? Just go and leave Tommofey to rule? Go back through the portal and live in peace with Lahnni and Evan, teaching Martial Arts to children and raising a family of his own?

Chapter 24

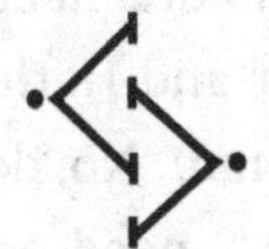

Samarra

Marra had looked everywhere but could not find her shoe. She held one in her hand, but the other was not to be found. She felt a building pressure and like the walls of the small room she stood in were pressing in on her. Shadows filled the corners, reminding her of assassins in masks that set her heart racing. Blood red flowers fell around her and the Branding symbols of the Gods flashed up on the walls in a random sequence, making the vivid dream even more confusing. Instead of trying to wake herself from this dream, Marra took in as much as she could. There was a message here; she just needed to figure out what it was. Or at least remember the details to write down and figure out later.

A door opened in the room she stood in, and she moved toward it, still holding her one shoe. The room beyond was full of whispering and held a dais with a throne split in two. The crown of Segarris lay in front of the throne, unclaimed, and the bodies of Harlonngraith and who she assumed was Tommofey lay at the base of the dais. Beyond the throne was a huge expanse of water and on it were hundreds of sails. She turned to see the shadowy figures of more assassin's creeping in through the door and screamed.

The scream in Marra's dream came out as a whimper, but enough to jolt her and Harley awake. He reached for her and began to hum. "No, don't," she said, pushing herself to sit upright. "I need pen and paper before I forget." This was one of those moments where she wished she had her mobile phone with her to quickly type in what she needed to remember.

She got out of bed and pulled on her robe. Harley did the same. "You find pen and paper, I'll get you more light," he said.

There had been a small writing desk set up in the corner for Harley to work at to continue to run his country from. Marra went to it and fumbled with the lid of the ink, her hands were a little shaky as her adrenaline had not settled. Harley placed the lamp he had lit on the desk and took the ink from her. "Here, let me. You still haven't mastered writing with quill and ink, it's probably best if I write it down."

"Fine, but don't ask questions, just write. I need to get it all out."

"Very well." He pulled out the chair and sat down, he looked up at her expectantly.

Marra began to talk. The missing shoe, the broken throne, the flashing symbols and what looked to be an invading navy. As many things as she could remember she told him about. "That's it," she said finally. "I don't know what it all means, but no matter what happens tomorrow, someone needs to know about this aside from us. Can you have a copy sent to Lopakka and Heiranni in the hope they might be able to divine something more from it?"

"Yes, I will see to it in the morning."

Marra paused and looked at her Bonded, she didn't know how he was going to respond to her next request but knew she needed to make it. "You must also tell your brother what I saw."

"Platisse?" he asked, a look of confusion on his face.

"No, Tommofey." His gray eyes widened but he didn't refuse. She went on. "If I die, that means you die, and it will be left to him to deal with whatever it all means. The people of Segarris need a King who is prepared."

"You will win—"

"I am not doing this with you now," Marra cut him off. "Promise me."

Harley looked at her and nodded his head. "I promise."

Chapter 25

Samarra

Arch Deacon Zussya was apologetic as he interrupted Marra and Harley's breakfast. "I am sorry to intrude, but there is much to be done this morning to adhere to the rules laid out for the Challengers and Champions." He walked into the private dining tent of the prince and his family and an ancient man and middle-aged woman followed behind him. This is Sister Innessa and Brother Arttem from the Orders charged to oversee this momentous event. They have already visited Prince Tommofey this morning," Zussya informed them all.

"Do not call him a prince, he has never been recognized," Anzhellika almost spat the words out as she slammed down her fork.

Marra noted that Harley's mother became incredibly irrational as soon as Darria or Tommofey were mentioned.

The Arch Deacon bowed his head in acknowledgment. "It is necessary until everything is determined. If he is a false prince and is refused entry to the Arena, Darria and Tommofey will pay the price immediately for their lies and false claims. There is a list of requirements that must be met and I have brought these two with me to take care of the first one."

The small, round Brother spoke briskly. "To be admitted into the Arena, the Champions must prove they are worthy. We are here to verify your Warrior brand."

Marra had to focus on each of his words as his accent was different to what she was used to. She nodded her agreement and came to stand before him and held out her right wrist to show him her tattoo.

He studied it for several moments and then looked up at her frowning. "What is the meaning of this?" he demanded.

Marra looked over to Harley. "What appears to be the problem?" He moved to stand next to her.

"Her brand is on the wrong wrist and doesn't look right."

This statement brought the attention of Sister Innessa, who had been eyeing the array of food rather than taking notice of the proceedings. "Let me see that."

Marra held out her wrist and allowed Sister Innessa to poke and prod the Warrior marking. "Why is it on that wrist? Is there something wrong with your other one?"

Marra hesitated and looked to Harley for guidance. "It's okay. Show them your other wrist."

Slowly she brought up her other arm and turned her hand over so her palm was face up, exposing her second tattoo. There was an audible gasp from both clergy people as they looked at the marking for the Gifted. "How is that possible?" Brother Arttem questioned.

"Is it even allowed?" muttered Sister Innessa.

"Of course, it is," announced a strong male voice as he entered the tent.

"Dad," Marra squealed as she hurried toward her father. She stopped for a moment as her mother entered behind him. It was like everyone in the room took a breath and held it. The Seer had returned.

Harley moved to stand before Kahlahnni and bowed before her. "Be welcome. I am pleased to have you here for Samarra's sake."

Her father looked at Marra critically before giving her a gentle hug. "You are injured," he whispered. It was not a question.

"Yes, assassins were sent," she murmured back as she kissed his cheek in greeting. There was no point in lying to him. "No one knows," Marra kissed his other cheek.

Nothing further was said as he made room for Kahlahnni to embrace her daughter. "I have missed you," Marra said softly as a feeling of unconditional love swept over her. It felt warm, and kind, and accepting. She wondered if it was her imagination and happiness at seeing her mother or something more now her mother had her full Seer powers back.

Kahlahnni spoke to the room but looked pointedly at Anzhellika. "Our time has come to return home. Many things will begin to be revealed and we are needed."

While everyone began to talk, Marra stepped outside and took in several breaths of fresh predawn air. So many people were depending on her, and in a few short hours it could all be over and she could have faltered and let them all down. It was a daunting thought and one she tried to keep at bay. Her ribs hurt as she took in a too deep breath, and she managed to stop herself from wincing. Marra had definitely broken one or two ribs when she had hit the ledge when fighting the assassins. She had wrapped them herself, claiming only bruising, but the pain had eased not as much as it should have over the past few weeks.

You just need to not die today, she told herself as she looked over at the massive stone structure, she had dreamed of months ago. *Just don't die.*

This story continues in

Fatal

Book 3

Right to Rule Series

The illegitimate son of a cast-off queen, Tommofey, has a score to settle.

Raised to believe he is the rightful heir to the throne of Segarris, Tommofey must now embark on his personal journey to find a Champion who will represent him when it comes time to challenge his half-brother, Harlonngraith, for the right to rule. He has been given a single clue from a suspect source—the supposed Seer of the Pomaikka—on where to begin his search. Should he take the risk and follow the word of someone who has been labelled a traitor?

Aviva worships her brother and is thrilled when she is reunited with him as he returns from the latest skirmishes upon the Islands of Lobbregath, but her joy is short lived when a stranger arrives and demands to see the most skilled swordsmen in the area. He promises riches beyond imagining for the right person. Aviva instantly dislikes him, but the money he offers would be enough for her and her brother to buy the small family farm they have always dreamed of owning. Is what this stranger promises too good to be true?

One wrong choice and the ending could be fatal for everyone.

A steamy enemies to lovers fantasy romance.

Excerpt from Fatal

Prince Tommofey rolled his eyes. "Are you slow, is there an issue with your learning? I will say this one more time, and then I am done with this conversation." He dragged out each word. "I am a prince. I can have any Servant I want assigned to me for no reason other than I wish it. I can have any soldier assigned to me on a whim. Do you understand what I am saying?"

"I am not an idiot; you do not need to be so condescending".

"Then stop behaving like one." He turned to leave.

"Wait, you haven't said what I will be doing for you." She didn't know why this was so important to her, but she kept pushing. He had told her she wouldn't be a camp follower so why did it matter?

He didn't bother to turn back but did pause in his exit. "You are a Servant. You will do chores."

"Such as?"

"God damn it, how would I know? Those matters are not my concern." The prince strode out the door.

"Arrogant prick," she muttered under her breath, smart enough to know that you didn't openly insult a prince, no matter your brand. Aviva stood there for several moments and an unexpected smile crossed her lips. There was something about that man that made her want to defy him just to see him lose his temper.

Warrior Brand

Religious Brand

Servant Brand

Commoner Brand

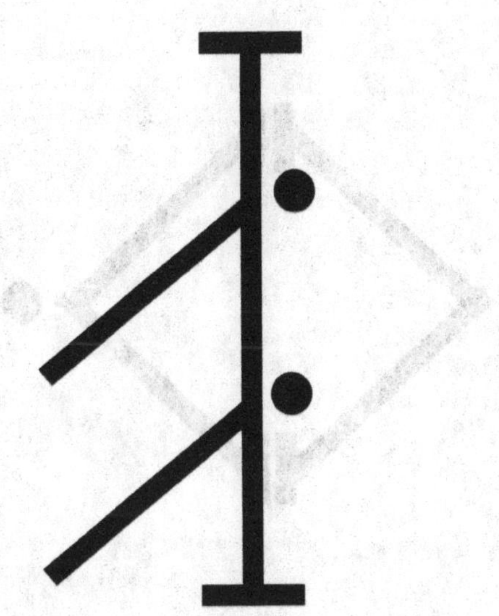

Roamer Brand

Gifted Brand

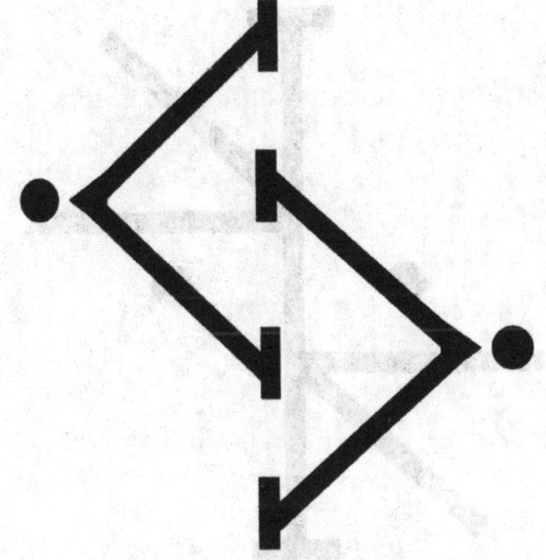

Noble Brand

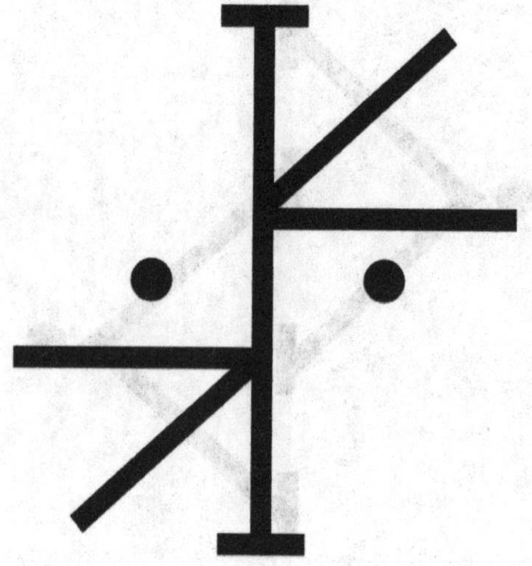

Monarch Brand

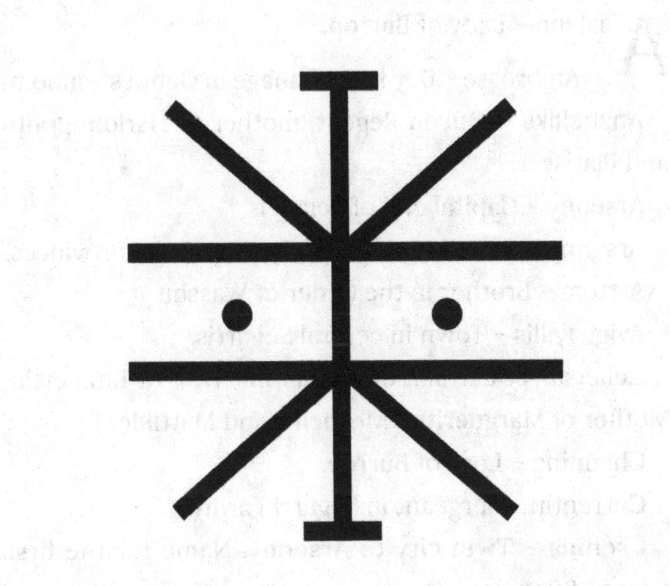

Glossary

Aislynn – Lady of Burrop.

Ambrosse – Boy in orphanage in Gennestenmont.

Anzhellika – Queen Regent, mother to Harlonngraith and Platisse.

Arsenny – Capital city of Segarris.

Arsenny – First King of Segarris, untied the Provinces.

Arttem – Brother in the Order of Wasshu.

Aviggayillis – Town in central Segarris.

Cellecia – Guardian of Kahlahnni. Wife of Emmettin. Mother of Margueritte, Mechelle, and Mattilde.

Channing – Lord of Burrop.

Correntin – Sergeant in Segarrin army.

Csennia – Twin city to Arsenny. Name for the first queen of Segarris.

Darria – Once Queen, now Lady. Mother to Tommofey.

Eltta – Pomaiikan instructor

Emmettin Finnley – Former Captain in Segarrin navy. Husband to Cellecia, father of Margueritte, Mechelle, and Mattilde. Guardian of Kahlahnni.

Evannderth Durrand – Sergeant, then Captain in the army of Segarris. Bonded to Kahlahnni, father of Samarra.

Gennestenmont – Town in northern province of Segarris.

Harlonngraith – First born son to King Tommofey and Queen Anzhellika.

Heiranni – Pomaikkan instructor for the Gifted. Father to Lopakka.

Innessa – Sister of the Order of Seggar.

Ittaie – General in Segarris army.

Jaggir – Religious Order.

Jaggiron – Northern Province of Segarris.

Jossiner – Laundry owner in Gennestenmont.

Kahlahnni – Seer of Segarris.

Lavee – Brother in the Order of Seggar.

Lopakka – Pomaikkan instructor for the Gifted. Son of Heiranni.

Marggot – Worked in laundry in Gennestenmont.

Margueritte – Eldest child of Cellecia and Emmettin. Sister of Mechelle and Mattilde.

Mattilde – Third born child of Cellecia and Emmettin. Sister of Margueritte and Mechelle.

Mechelle – Second child of Cellecia and Emmettin. Sister of Margueritte and Mattilde.

Moehanne – Pomaikkan word for Soul Sleeper.

Ohanelle – Pomaikkan of the Settlement.

Peggy – Evannderth's maid in the palace.

Platisse – Second born son to King Tommofey and Queen Anzhellika. Brother of Harlonngraith and Tommofey.

Pluddgish – Main Outpost Island of Lobbregath

Pomaikka – A race of people.

Pressac – Town in northern province.

Roamer – Common name for Pomaikkan.

Ruby – Kahlahnni's Horse.

Saffed – Forest where the Challenger Arena is.

Samarra – Daughter of Kahlahnni and Evannderth. Soul Sleeper of Segarris. Champion to Prince Harlongraith.

Seggar – Religious Order.

Segarris – A Country.

Sittiq – Brother in the Order of Seggar.

Seer – A Gift given by the Gods.

Soul Sleeper – A Gift given by the Gods.

Tommofey – Former King of Segarris.

Tommofey – Third born son to King Tommofey, first born to Lady Darria. Half-brother to Harlonngraith and Platisse.

Traiss – Inn Keeper's daughter in Gennestenmont.

Trioswa – Nation that invades Islands of Lobbregath.

Wasshu – Religious Order.

Wasshun – Eastern Province of Segarris.

Zussya – Arch Deacon of the Order of Seggar.

About Taya Rune

Taya Rune is a writer of romance, a sucker for happy endings, and has a knack for asking people uncomfortable questions.

She is a USA Today Bestselling Author and a finalist for the 2022 Romantic Book of the Year, for the Romance Writer's of Australia RuBY awards. She has had her work published in many different anthologies and publications.

Romantic Women's Fiction

Reflections of Love Collection
Also releasing on Radish and available in Audio format

Hannah

Samantha

Olivia

Chloe

Lacy

Grace

Reflections of Love Novella Collection Volume 1

(Contains books 1 – 4)

For more information on all titles head to tayarune.com

Acknowledgments

I would like to take a few moments
to say thank you.

To my children, thank you for
teaching me to let go of the small stuff. I am proud of you.

To my family, thank you for the
love and support you have shown me throughout the
years.

To my friends, the ones that have
my back and are forever in my corner – I cherish you.

To my editor, Rochelle J. Simas – IDK art.
Thank you for the kind words that
always accompany the return of my fabulously edited
manuscripts.

To my ARC, Street, Beta, and Proofreader Teams.
You are appreciated.

Follow her on your favorite platform:

Website:
https://www.tayarune.com

Facebook:
https://www.facebook.com/taya.rune.75

Facebook Group:
https://www.facebook.com/groups/tayasromanticreal
m

Instagram:
https://www.instagram.com/tayarune/

Bookbub:
https://www.bookbub.com/authors/taya-rune

Goodreads:
https://www.goodreads.com/author/show/21156065.T
aya_Rune

Pinterest:
https://www.pinterest.com.au/TayaRune

Taya Rune